A PLAGUE OF UNICORNS

A Selection of Middle Grade Books by Jane Yolen

Snow in Summer

B.U.G. (Big Ugly Guy)

Centaur Rising

The Devil's Arithmetic

The Transfigured Hart

The Young Merlin Trilogy

Passager

Hobby

Merlin

A PLAGUE OF UNICORNS

NEW YORK TIMES BESTSELLING AUTHOR

JANE YOLEN

ZONDERkidz

ZONDERKIDZ

A Plague of Unicorns

This title is also available as a Zondervan ebook.
Visit www.zondervan.com/ebooks

Requests for information should be addressed to:
Zonderkidz, *3900 Sparks Drive SE, Grand Rapids, Michigan 49546*

This edition: ISBN 978-0-310-74611-9 (softcover)

Library of Congress Cataloging-in-Publication Data

Yolen, Jane.
A plague of unicorns / by Jane Yolen.
pages cm
"This novel is based on the short story 'An Infestation of Unicorns,' by Jane Yolen, from Here There Be Unicorns, 1994."
Summary: James, an earl's son and bothersome child, may hold the key to saving Cranford Abbey, a dilapidated school where he is sent to be educated, that newly-appointed Abbot Aelian thinks can be saved if he can make cider from the golden apples now being eaten by ravenous unicorns.
ISBN 978-0-310-74648-5 (hardcover)
ISBN 978-0-310-74611-9 (softcover)
ISBN 978-0-310-74610-2 (epub)
[1. Boarding schools—Fiction. 2. Schools—Fiction. 3. Unicorns—Fiction. 4. Heroes—Fiction.] I. Title.
PZ7.Y78Pl 2015
[Fic]—dc23 2014016576

Cover design: Jody Langley
Cover illustration: John Rowe
Interior illustration: Tom McGrath
Interior design: Matthew Van Zomeren

Printed in the United States of America

---

15 16 17 18 19 20 21 22 23 24 25 /DCI/ 14 13 12 11 10 9 8 7 6 5 4 3 2 1

For my youngest granddaughters—
Caroline and Amelia—and all the unicorns
to come. Plus a special thanks to my oldest
granddaughter, Glendon Alexandria Callan,
whose name I have borrowed and
who has always been my hero.

This novel is based on Jane Yolen's short story "An Infestation of Unicorns" from her book *Here There Be Unicorns*, illustrated by David Wilgus (New York: Harcourt Brace, 1994). The poem "The Making of the Unicorn" (used for the epigraph) is from *Here There Be Unicorns* as well.

The Making of the Unicorn

Take this bone, this ivory,
This slender pyramid, this spear,
This walking stick, this cornucopia,
This twisted instrument of fear,
This mammoth tusk, this pearly thorn,
This mythic spike, this maiden's bier,
This denticle, this rib of time,
This alabaster harrow—here
We start the beast, we give it name.
The world will never be the same.

1

IN WHICH WE ARE INTRODUCED TO A SHORT HISTORY OF THE UNICORN PLAGUE

In one of the orchards behind the high stone walls of Cranford Abbey grew five different varieties of apple trees.

Three varieties bore ordinary green and red apples, which the monks had named Plainsong, Nones, and Prime.

One variety of tree bore apples the deep purple of port wine. The priests called them Sanctus.

And one group of trees bore apples that were a startling gold, a color that would put mustard to shame and make wheat weep, if such were possible. The first abbot of the abbey had cried "*Hosannah!*" That's a shout of praise, from the Latin, which is a language abbots, monks, and priests know well. His shout was heard by all the monks laboring in the orchard, and the name stuck.

The unicorns dined only on the golden Hosannah apples when they came through Cranford on their fall migration. They left the other apples quite alone.

No one remembered when they'd first come through the abbey grounds. There were only two mentions of them in the abbey records. One had been an offhand reference to "the white beast, the glory of God" in one of the long-misplaced hymn books. The other reference was a picture, rather smudged, of a unicorn eating an apple in the middle of the garden of Eden, in an illuminated manuscript about the wild beasts of Britannia.

For years no one had disturbed the unicorns at their feast. A lone unicorn may be a magnificent animal, full of rare enchantment and beauty. However, in a herd they

can prove exceedingly cranky and exceptionally dangerous if disturbed, especially if they are disturbed while eating golden apples.

Now the first abbot, and the second, and the third—all fine and holy men—were long gone to their heavenly reward at the time of this story. They had each suffered the unicorns to share the golden apples, with only a few apples left at the end of the autumn at the topmost of each tree. For as the first abbot wrote in the Abbot's Journal, "There are but few golden apple trees in the orchard, and those trees are far from the others." And the second abbot added that, "The golden apples are not particularly plump nor pleasing to the tongue." And the third had said, definitively, "Not worth the battle."

But then the fourth abbot was appointed. Abbot Aelian was a tall, greying man with a face that seemed to be considering everything—monks, tapestries, suppers, silver—and always finding them wanting. He had served as abbot of a smaller abbey in France, and spoke many languages, including owl—or so the French monks believed, for he could whistle and call down owls on Christmas Eve.

Abbot Aelian walked the halls of Cranford as silent as a ghost, but he had the gift of Presence when he wanted to be seen. He brought with him a recipe for apple cider that had been in his family for generations, a recipe for Golden Apple Cider.

He went around and about the abbey those first days, checking it from foundation to attic, from the walled gardens to the great compost heaps steaming in the sun. Nothing eluded his searching eyes. He checked the well, the hearths both large and small, the two spits for roasting, and the old dungeon where faulty parts of equipment were stored. He spent an entire morning noodling about in the big abbey kitchen, lifting lids, tasting the soup, testing the strength of every kettle, making lists of all the stores in the larder and the cold cellar. But he never smiled.

"He's not so much an abbot as a counting-house man," complained Brother Gregory, the cook, to anyone who would listen. He shook his fat forefinger as he spoke. "Mark my words, he will do nothing for the abbey or us monks."

In his tour of the abbey, Abbot Aelian learned that the stone walls had been breached in a number of places. The roof of the main building leaked, and was especially bad over the scriptorium, where monks worked tirelessly to illuminate pages of the Bible. To save the manuscripts and scrolls from the dripping ceiling, many monks had long since moved their individual desks to their individual cells so they might continue their work of decorating manuscripts with colorful capital letters and illustrations both beautiful and odd.

Also, alas, quite a few of the stained glass windows had been broken due to unseasonal hail. In fact, in one of the windows detailing the Crucifixion, Barabbas—the prisoner who'd been pardoned—had disappeared from his pane of glass entirely, leaving only an unfurled banner with his name on it.

Abbot Aelian returned to the kitchen at the end of the tour. He was carrying three large soup pots. "These are yours, I gather," he said to Brother Gregory. "We cannot have your good cook pots serving as drip catchers. Especially now that many of the monks are working on their illuminations in their own cells." He nodded at Brother Gregory but did not smile as he handed the pots over. "Their own cells are uncomfortable at best, and, I fear, not a very welcoming work space. That needs sorting immediately and will solve two things at once—the scriptorium and the pots in your fine kitchen."

Brother Gregory immediately stopped his complaining and became the abbot's friend for as long as they both lived, which—as it turned out—was well into their nineties.

Between them, Brother Gregory and the abbot went about testing the Golden Cider recipe on themselves and some trusted cook boys. They'd tried the other apples first, hoping to use the varieties already in abundant supply, but the cider always seemed to lack something: one was too sweet, one too sour, one too musty, one too sharp.

There was only a handful of the golden Hosannahs left from the last plague of unicorns. They had been at the tip top of the trees, left there when the unicorns had departed. The youngest of the monks had gone up on ladders and taken the few golden apples down, hurrying back with them to the kitchen. Seventeen apples in all. They were not good eating apples, nor good baking apples, and Brother Gregory was more than willing to use them in a cider test. But there were not enough for a full sampling by the monks. He was only able to make enough to fill two medium-sized mugs.

However, two medium-sized mugs was enough for anyone who took part in the test, for even a drop of the drink tasted *heavenly*. That was the word that all the tasters agreed upon.

It was hoped that the sale of the cider from these apples would help restore Cranford Abbey. Or, as the abbot said when he called the monks together in the small sanctuary of the abbey church, "The sale of cider has saved many an abbey in France. With my great-great-grandmother's recipe and the magnificent Hosannahs we have here in the abbey garden, there is no reason why we cannot restore Cranford to its former glory."

The monks cheered, and one of the youngest of the oblates turned three cartwheels in the aisle, much to the delight of his friends—though it won him a hard look from Brother David, who taught them mathematics and art and was said to smile once a year whether he meant it or not.

"Now," said the abbot, "about those unicorns. I have a plan."

Everyone cheered again, though some of the older monks were rather hesitant when it came to applause. They had been through this before.

So, in that first autumn of Aelian's rule, when the golden apples were at their ripest, the battle lines were drawn—monks against unicorns.

It was not a fair fight, because the monks believed that to harm any animal except for the purposes of dinner was wrong. Further, they believed that harming a unicorn—thought to be the animal avatar of the Christ—brought about the greatest of misfortunes.

Besides, they had no weapons but Brother Gregory's three large knives, which he was reluctant to give up as easily as he had given up his pots.

The unicorns, as far as was known, had no such thoughts about monks. And, besides, they had very sharp horns.

Here ends the first part of the Short History of the Unicorn Plague.

2

THE SHORT HISTORY OF THE UNICORN PLAGUE, PART TWO

At the end of that first autumn encounter—"The Abbot's War," as it was called in the town of Cranford—the tally stood as such:

Burly Brother Alford—pierced through the hand.

Skinny Father Emmanuel—run through the thigh.

Two novices with turned ankles from scampering away.

One oblate with a skinned knee, having fallen out of a tree where the unicorns fed.

Three infant oblates—young boys given to the abbey as toddlers by their parents—awaking each night with screaming nightmares.

And the unicorns?

No casualties or injuries. In fact, the leader had begun taunting Abbot Aelian, letting him get closer, closer, and then trotting away with a toss of his head and a whinny that sounded remarkably like a laugh. The golden apples? Except for the topmost apples—all gone.

In the town of Cranford, which lay to the immediate west of the abbey and its gardens, the locals began to make jokes about what had happened.

"To fight an apple-bapple" meant "to wage an uneven contest."

"Apple pudding" was something frightened children did in their pants.

"As rare as a golden apple in the Lord Abbot's garden" meant something that didn't exist at all.

Boys invented bouncing ball rhymes, such as:

See the monks all in a row.
In come the unicorns ... down they go.

Girls made up skip-rope tunes:

Abbot, Abbot, say your prayers,
I hear a unicorn on the stairs.

Abbot Aelian was not amused by any of this. He felt the entire countryside was laughing at the abbey, and especially at him—and he was right. Though he was a good man, he had absolutely no sense of humor. Or so it was thought.

And he had no golden apples to make his cider, either.

That winter Abbot Aelian studied the unicorns out of his tower window as they devoured the golden assets of the garden, and he began to devise a plan. He read all about unicorns in three great books of unicorn anatomy that the abbey owned: *The Unicornus Is a Wily Beast* was the thinnest of the volumes, and he tackled that first. Next he read *De Natura Unicorni* in Latin, and finally he tried *Unicornis in Tribulo*, but found it too fantastic for his liking.

"A romance more than a treatise," as he explained to Brother Luke over his tea. Brother Luke, short and stout, had the finest hand at illuminations, and so he and the abbot had tea every other day to discuss the books in the library and the ones being worked on by the monks.

Brother Luke nodded. He liked romances more than treatises himself, but he wasn't about to admit that to the abbot.

Abbot Aelian understood from both observation and research that unicorns took one week to eat all they could, one week to digest what they could, and one week to excrete what was left. And then they started eating all over again. He read that part of the *De Natura* to Brother Luke and was delighted when the round monk smiled and nodded in return.

"So it is with many animals," Brother Luke said. "Though horses eat and excrete rather more quickly."

"Lucky then," said the abbot, "that we are dealing with unicorns."

"Lucky indeed," replied Brother Luke.

So the second autumn, Abbot Aelian set his tallest, strongest monks to guard the gates into the orchards while the infant oblates and novitiates were to hide in the branches of the red and green apple trees as lookouts.

"We need only to keep them out one week in three," the abbot said.

He allowed his "holy warriors," as he called the monks, to carry pitchforks for protection, as well as kitchen cloths to snap at the unicorns' backsides. He gave each of the two priests slingshots purchased from the town, plus a full cloth pocket of hard peas to use as ammunition. The oblates and novitiates—or at least the most capable of the boys—he posted in the actual Hosannah trees because they were the lightest and would not break any branches. They were supplied with buckets of warm water fortified by fish guts to rain down upon the beasts, because in one of the books the abbot had read, such a combination was called "Unicorn Bane," meaning that unicorns hated it and would run away at even the slightest whiff.

The holy warriors practiced their maneuvers all winter long. The priests with the slings started acting like boys. And the oblates all got soaking wet and came in smelling dreadfully of fish guts.

The longer they practiced, the more problems arose. The towel-snappers began snapping anyone walking quietly in the *dortoir*, the dormitory where they all lived. Those they pounced upon ran away screaming, which violated all of the abbey's rules on silence.

As for the pitchfork brigade, they were lucky not to run one another through, though it was a close thing.

And three of the boys — Bartholomew, Aiden, and George — got soaking wet once too often in the deep cold of winter and came down with walkabout pneumonia, forcing them to stay in bed with warm compresses for days on end.

The abbot gathered all of the members of his abbey family together one evening after prayers. It was close to Christmas, and he gave them what would be written down as his Christmas homily, though it was less about God and more about the unicorns.

"My children," he began, looking down on them from the high pulpit, "God does not want you to overtax yourselves in this practice, nor to make yourselves ill. This is but a rehearsal only. Save your real bravado for when the beasts actually arrive again in the fall."

Bartholomew, Aiden, and George — who had bonded in the infirmary — had quite enjoyed overtaxing themselves and then having to take it easy in the soft infirmary beds. They liked being read to as they lay in a half stupor. It wouldn't be hard to do it all over again as soon as the abbot would let them. They winked at one another and nodded their heads.

Then Bartholomew whispered, "We'll get them next time, boys!" Meaning, of course, the unicorns.

Few of the ordinary duties besides prayer got done that cold winter.

By March, everyone at the abbey, except Bartholomew and his boys, was exhausted by the unicorn practice, even as modest as it had become. And as Brother Luke cautioned, "They are not practiced in anything now but boredom."

So Abbot Aelian allowed them to rest up all spring and summer with only minor practices.

For the monks and most of the novices, it was a relief to return to the scriptorium or the kitchen or the winter gardening or the animal care—the goats and the cows had suffered the most from neglect. And there were the bell ringing duties and the washing of the stone floors.

But for the oblates—especially Bartholomew, Aiden, and George—it was a return to a life of order and silence, the hardest thing for young boys to endure. So they practiced at night, in secret, and had to be wakened rudely with a hearty shake each morning by the monk in charge.

The gardening monks still kept a careful eye on the orchard trees, of course. It was their job. They watched the flowers first, then the buds, then the hard bead of each small apple. They reported what was happening every day to Abbot Aelian, who wrote it down in a notebook labeled *Of the Labors of Gardeners*. It was, he hoped, to be his greatest work. After defeating the unicorns, of course.

The gardeners and their novices waited impatiently, then fearfully, then hopefully as the apple beads of late summer grew large and round, and it was clear they were nearing a major harvest.

They hoped that after the slingshots and fish guts and the rest, the unicorns had decided to go elsewhere.

And just when they were congratulating themselves on a job well done, and the bell ringers were ringing out the canonical hours, the unicorns came back, threading their way across the meadows of barley towards the orchard.

It was Bartholomew who saw them first from his perch in the tallest Plainsong apple tree. He sang out his discovery in a voice that mixed pride with a dash of bravado and a pinch of fear.

Here ends the second part of the Short History of the Unicorn Plague.

3

THE SHORT HISTORY OF THE UNICORN PLAGUE, PART THREE

That fall's battle was worse than the first.

Unicorns are wily animals, or so it says in the bestiaries. The monks discovered this for themselves. They watched as the unicorns leaped like goats over fences and noted how they smelled out traps as cannily as badgers. And it seemed the unicorns were no longer afraid of either towels or pitchforks. They also appeared to love the warm water bane. Though they were, perhaps, not wild about the fish guts.

The abbot watched out his window again

and despaired. He saw white beast after white beast evading all the traps the monks had set for them. He saw boys tumble from the trees and have to limp away before they were trampled by those fierce hooves.

And one boy landed on top of a unicorn and proceeded to try to ride it around the orchard, being dislodged at the last minute and nearly losing a limb to the infuriated unicorn's horn. Abbot Aelian thought it was Bartholomew, though from so far away he couldn't be sure.

Only the boy's natural instinct of preservation, plus the fact he rolled into the orchard's swift river and was recovered downstream by some of the older monks, saved him from more than just another bout of pneumonia.

It turned out it was Bartholomew, and as he told the story of what happened, he made it even better, speaking of the unicorn's bugling call of surprise when Bartholomew landed on his back. How the unicorn bucked like a charger when it first feels the weight of a saddle. How the unicorn snorted stars out its nose. Bartholomew made up a lot of it. Well, really, all of it, but in doing so became the hero of all of the boys.

Now unicorns, as Abbot Aelian had read in the three books in the abbey's library, can only be captured by a pure maiden with a golden halter. And a maiden—as any fool can tell you—is never allowed in a monastery or on monastery land. No girls. None. Never. It's an absolute rule.

Perhaps that was why the unicorns felt so

safe doing their apple thievery in an abbey garden, while leaving alone any golden apples that grew at castles and great houses. Or perhaps the Cranford apples were just too perfect and wonderful to resist.

Besides, what Abbot Aelian had not fully calculated was that if his barely trained army of monks, priests, novitiates, and oblates kept the unicorns from the garden one week, they would simply enter it the next. It was a kind of sliding scale. (But in the abbot's defense, sliding scales had not yet been invented.)

Anyway, the count after the second fall's battle was this:

One priest and four novitiates injured, though only the priest had to spend time in the surgery.

Three infant oblates with screaming nightmares, who had to be sent home to their mothers.

Young Bartholomew in the infirmary with a coughing sickness that the infirmerer feared might turn into pleurisy.

Abbot Aelian was forced to ask for help.

After that fall battle, the monks in the scriptorium (and the ones at work in their own cells) had to stop illuminating Bibles and prayer books to crank out about a hundred fancy posters to be tacked on walls around the countryside.

Each poster was decorated with famous encounters with animals from Scripture, the most popular being Samson's slaying his enemies with the jawbone of a donkey, Jonah in the whale's belly, and the ram caught in the thicket where Isaac was bound. Only Mary entering Bethlehem on a donkey and the Gadarene swine were left out.

That is why, in the third autumn of Aelian's rule, heroes flocked to the abbey's door, the line of them sometimes winding all the way around to the outer walls.

"Who knew," the abbot mused, "that heroes grew so abundantly in the kingdom."

"Not just *our* kingdom," grumbled Father Joseph, who tended to the abbey stores. "They have come from as far away as Caledonia and across the seas from Gaul, Germania, Afrik, Cathay, and Rome."

The heroes came in all shapes and sizes, mostly big.

Nearly a hundred heroes in all.

They spoke languages as diverse as Aramaic, Latin, Mandarin, Pictish, Doric, and Greek. They wore armor or togas or tartans

or albs or practically nothing at all. They carried swords, bows, spears, pikes, nunchakus, and slings.

Father Joseph, who looked hawkish and sunken, made lists of the heroes, and then he made lists of the lists. He mumbled all day long and in his sleep as well. He was not a happy man. For even when—at his insistence—the posters were taken down, the heroes kept arriving.

"There must be an underground hero network," he whispered to his best friend in the abbey, Father John. They looked alike

and sounded alike, though Father John was a full head shorter than Father Joe.

"One tells another, tells another," Father John whispered back.

"I wonder what they say," Father Joseph replied.

"Probably that we serve good food."

"And apples." This last was said in a growl. Father Joseph's patience was near its end. "I will tell the abbot we must stop feeding the heroes, lest we have nothing for ourselves come next year."

But Abbot Aelian was not moved by Father Joseph's arguments. He insisted on giving each hero a large dinner and an equally large breakfast for three days of hero-work—which further used up the abbey's stores.

Father Joseph kept careful count and did not stop complaining to Father John.

The first of the heroes to arrive was Sir Geoffrey of Stonewait Manor, who sat on a horse with feet the size of dinner plates.

Sir Geoffrey pounded on the door. He

looked much like a hero with long, flowing golden locks, and arms the size of tree trunks.

"He will do," Abbot Aelian said with a small smile.

Sir Geoffrey sat at dinner with the abbot. In between devouring an entire haunch of lamb, three chickens stewed in sherry, and a dessert of apple cobbler, he told the abbot his plan.

"For combat with a single unicorn," he said, the words hard to make out between his moustache and his full mouth, "a sword will do. As long as it has a farther reach than the creature's horn." He piled two apple cobblers on his plate, then tucked into both of them. "I am your man, abbot."

But the next morning, after a huge breakfast, and after he'd gone into the orchard with his newly sharpened sword, Sir Geoffrey came back white-faced and shaking.

"You did not say it was a *herd* of unicorns," he said, reaching for a flagon of apple cider. "A single hero cannot possibly face all of them. You need an army of swords standing in porcupine formation."

Father Joseph shook his head miserably, thinking of feeding an army at the abbey.

"Or a maiden," Sir Geoffrey said. "Unicorns will follow a maiden, you know."

"No maidens allowed here," the abbot retorted. "No females," he said. "Not young or old. This is an abbey. That's the rule."

So Sir Geoffrey left, a bag full of scones for his long trip home cadged from Father Joseph, who was delighted to see him go.

About fifty useless heroes later, the extra-large Sir Humphrey Hippomus of Castle Dire showed up on a horse whose feet were like soup tureens.

He, too, ate his way through a massive dinner and a bigger breakfast, then went off to fight a single unicorn with a pike. "Because," as he told the abbot, "my pike is bigger than the unicorn's spike. It's simply size that wins in the end."

But like Sir Geoffrey before him, Sir Humphrey came back shaking, white-faced, and thirsty. He downed three flagons of the regular apple cider before saying, "That wasn't *one* unicorn. It wasn't a herd. It was a *horde* of the beasts. You need an army in the porcupine formation."

"No army here," Abbot Aelian said. "Monks are a people of peace. That's the rule."

Father Joseph and Father John counted up the cost, and Father John walked out of the countinghouse shaking his head. Already it was too high, and still the unicorns ate the fruit.

Fifty or so even *more* useless heroes came and went before the extra-extra-large Sir Sullivan Gallivant of the Long Barrow arrived. Sir Sullivan was too big for any horse, so he rode in a tumbrel pulled by a pair of matched drays.

He waddled into the entry hall, ate in the larder, and devoured a half day's supply of food before getting back into his cart.

"I'll bring you back the head of yon unicorn," he said. "*Nae* problem."

His nae was very loud, and he sounded

like a horse himself. He shook his bow in the direction of the orchard.

The cart made rumbling, tumbling noises as it left, and even louder noises as it returned just a few minutes later.

"I've only ten arrows," shouted Sir Sullivan, his voice a thunder, "and there must be a hundred head of unicorns there!"

"A hundred and seventy-two, by last count," mumbled Father Joseph.

"Plus or minus," added Father John.

The abbot said, "Bring him a flagon of cider," and one of the monks raced out with it.

Before they could thank him for his try, he'd turned the cart around and was gone, calling back over his shoulder, "Try a brace of cannons!"

"No cannons allowed here," the abbot retorted. "Only canon law," he added, almost smiling at his own small joke. He was not much given to joking. "That's the rule."

Father Joseph said to Father John, "He's taken the flagon with him."

Father John shrugged. "Even though the chalice is silver, it is worth the price to have him gone. He would have eaten the rest of our stores if given a chance."

Soon after that, all the heroes left, having eaten their way through hundreds of pounds of food, having left their trash and carried away treasures, and their horses having trampled the grass around the orchard into a muddy bog. In their own way, the heroes were as bad as the unicorns.

Maybe even worse.

Difficult as the heroes were, with no more in sight, Abbot Aelian was distressed. His prayers seemed unanswered, and he began to question whether he should just leave the unicorns to their destructive ways unchecked.

"Perhaps," he said to Father Joseph, "the Lord wants the abbey to fail."

"If he wanted the abbey to fail," Father Joseph said softly, "he would not have sent you here to us."

The abbot nodded. "But I am out of ideas."

"But not out of prayers," said Father

Joseph, and they went back into the sanctuary to pray.

Now, it's not written down what the two of them prayed for, but surely it wasn't for an eight-year-old boy, the heir to a dukedom, with a smudge on his nose. They would both have laughed roundly at that. That is, if they'd been laughing men.

But sometimes a little child *can* lead.

4

In Which James Asks Too Many Questions and Gets Too Few Answers

About fifty miles from the abbey sat Castle Callander, where the nearby Callan River twisted sluggishly like an old dragon. The castle had seven turrets that reached fists towards the sky. It had long, many-paned, corbelled windows, arrow slits left over as defense from the many earlier wars, and a dry moat. The grey stone was worn in places but still had many years to go before parts had to be replaced. And the Duke of Callanshire's banner—a red dragon rampant—

flew on a high flagpole whenever the family was at home. And they were *always* at home.

In the castle dwelt the Duke of Callanshire, his wife, the Duchess Ann, their daughter, Alexandria, their son and heir, eight-and-a-half-year-old James, and baby Bruce.

Callanshire was a lovely land of vast fields and dense forests, of rolling hills and acres of farmland. The shire was divided into three counties: Callan itself, which was where the castle stood; East Riding, where the abbey was situated; and Hockney, where the big market towns crowded together like pigs at a trough.

Though some distance from Hockney, the castle was close enough to the abbey for the heirs of the dukedom to be educated there, but far enough away so that gossip did not fly between.

That was why no one at Castle Callander had heard about the plague of unicorns at the abbey. Or if they had, they thought it merely a minstrel's tale.

On this morning, the heir to the dukedom, James—who was almost nine years old—

was sharing the breakfast with his mother and his sister, Alexandria. The baby was upstairs in the nursery with Nanny. He was still too young to eat downstairs and would be for some time. Bruce was his name, or The Baby. Though he was sometimes called "The Spare," because if something should happen to James, Bruce would become the next heir.

James didn't worry about any of that. He didn't worry about much. Worry would come later.

James peered at his mother from under his mop of white-gold hair. His eyes were the sharp blue of a spring sky. He and his mother shared the same color eyes and hair, and they shared the same fierce intelligence.

Alexandria was even smarter, but not nearly as blonde, and her eyes were a kind of grey, like Spanish steel. Her mother used to say that Alexandria's spine must be made of steel, too, for she was as straight and true as a well-made sword.

The thing most people noticed first about James was that mop of hair, then the sharp blue eyes, and the fact that he was still missing an upper tooth on either side of his upper mouth—which gave it the look of the castle portcullis. He never seemed to be still, but was a running, tumbling boy who was forever exploring. "His nose," his father used to say, "leads him like a hound on the hunt."

For the most part, James was a tidy boy. Except when he forgot to wash behind his ears. And there was often a smudge on his nose, which Nanny or his mother or Alexandria used to wipe off with a quick rub from a ready cloth. A "clootie," Nanny called her cloth, because she was from Caledonia, a cold and inhospitable land some said, but not Nanny, who planned to retire there.

But the thing that most people remembered about James was that he asked questions. All the time. By nature, he was extremely curious. He had long ago tired out everyone in the castle with his questions. They had all grown *Weary of Query*, as Alexandria had aptly said.

At this particular morning meal, he was engaged in questioning his mother. He had already asked her in quick succession, "Why does the sun rise in the morning? Is it like one of Cook's cakes? What are its ingredients?" And then pointing to the eggs on his plate, and without stopping to draw breath, he asked, "Are these duck eggs or goose eggs? Can they lay spotted eggs as well?"

He didn't notice the lines growing between his mother's eyes, a clear sign she was annoyed. Nor did he give her time to answer any of his questions before adding, "When will Father be home?"

She looked at him, seemed like she was

about to say something, then turned her face away.

Alexandria put her hand on his. "Hush," she said. "There are some questions that should not be asked."

At that, the duchess looked back. Her eyes were shining oddly. "Your father has disappeared in the Holy Lands. Perhaps on his own Crusade. Perhaps following the Saviour's footsteps. Perhaps dead and buried in the sand. We have sent men to find out what has happened. But if you are to be the next Duke of Callanshire presently, you must learn to school your thoughts." Her voice was steady, but her eyes shone now with tears. She did not let them drop.

"But," James said, filling the room with more questions, since it felt as if all the air had suddenly rushed out of it, "if Father is on his own Crusade, is it dangerous? And if he is following the Saviour's footsteps, will they lead him to the Crucifixion? And if . . . and if . . ." He finally ran out of queries.

His mother looked at him deeply, as if she understood everything he was feeling, everything he was trying to say. But instead of putting a comforting arm around him, she said simply, "Go tell Nanny you've got another smudge, and tell her I said your face needs washing."

Which he did, without asking her another question, without thinking about anything, and especially not thinking about the unshed tears in her eyes.

In the nursery, baby Bruce was just getting up from his morning nap, or just arising from his night sleep. It was hard to tell which. He slept a lot.

James asked Nanny, "Do all babies sleep this much, or just our Bruce?"

Nanny snapped, "*You* didn't sleep at all!"

But if she thought that would stop James, she was mistaken. "Why do some babies sleep all the time and others not at all? Is it because they have different lullabies in their blood? Or is it a sign of goodness? Or badness? Or—"

"Talking too much is a sign of a slovenly

mind," Nanny said. "That smudge on the side of your nose is another." And holding baby Bruce in one arm, she attacked James' nose with a clootie until he felt scrubbed raw of skin and of questions.

Finally managing to wiggle away from Nanny's fierce attentions and baby Bruce's drools, James went outside.

But where to go? Nanny, Cook, all the housemaids, the stableman who worked with the horses, the dog-boy who cared for the hounds, the blacksmith who shoed the horses and made swords and belt buckles for the soldiers as well as knives for the kitchen, the ten soldiers, and Master Henry who taught them swordsmanship—they all tended to look very busy whenever James got near. In fact, they turned their backs or bent over their tasks or marched in the other direction rather than engage with him. So he had very few people to talk to, which caused him to have an even greater store of unanswered questions.

Even his succession of tutors had run

from him. In fact, every single one had quit in the last two years because of the incessant queries. Including his father, who—he was sure—went off on Crusade mostly to get away from him. In fact, the next-to-last thing his father had said before leaving on his great roan horse was, "James, cultivate silence. It will serve you well." And then he added, "You are a good son, so mind your manners, say your prayers, and keep yourself to yourself." And then he was gone.

Yes, thought James, *everyone ignores me or runs away from me.* Well, except Alexandria, and his latest tutor, Benedict Cumber.

("Cumbersome!" Alexandria had called him, and it had stuck.)

Cumbersome had been around less than two months, brought in after the last tutor had gone, slamming the door behind him—a heavy door that made a very large bang—and shouting, "Thank the Lord! No more questions!"

At first Cumbersome had paid a lot of attention to James—Master James he called him, and "sir," which the other tutors had not. But question after question seemed to have worn the man down as well. James was pretty sure Cumbersome was already tired of him.

James thought about the day before, when the two of them had been in the library. James was supposedly studying his geography and was stuck on the countries bordering France. They seemed to move around and change names a lot.

"How can a country change its name?" James had asked Cumbersome. "Can I change my name? I'd like to be Forrest or Merrie or—"

"Look at the globe, Master James," Cumbersome had said dryly. "It will tell you what you need to know."

Everything about Cumbersome is dry, James thought. *Even his nose never runs.* (James' nose ran all the time.)

"If you wouldn't ask so many questions," Cumbersome added, "you would find a whole lot more answers on your own." It was something the duke had often said, and so James was startled into a moment of silence.

But at last he sighed and said to Cumbersome, "If I didn't ask questions, how would I know when I had the wrong answers?"

Cumbersome rolled his eyes and went out of the room, leaving James alone with the globe.

"Globe," James said, "why are you round?"

The globe, of course, didn't answer.

Cumbersome's leaving the room hadn't surprised James. Everyone in the castle hastened away from him. Most of them even before he'd opened his mouth.

As if, he thought, *my questions walk before me, and I am but their shadow.* It was not a comforting thought.

The gardeners—there were four of them, a father and his three sons—all suddenly found important work to do whenever James came down the path.

"The young heir can be maddening with his questions," advised the head gardener to his boys. "He asks questions he doesn't need to know the answers for, like, 'Do roses come in black for funerals?' and, 'Are caterpillars useful for more than making butterflies?' If you are not careful, he could pull you away from an entire day of work."

The gardener's youngest son, a boy called Weed, agreed. "He asked me once if I really had a green thumb," Weed said. "I had to take off my glove to show him it was just like his. I think he was disappointed in me, Da."

The maids had orders not to speak to James, for it was hard to escape a lengthy conversation with him once it started. Besides, he asked the oddest things, like, "Why do maids dust things when it's dust they should be removing?"

But even the maids who liked to tease James had to get on with their work. So they just put their hands over their mouths and giggled if they had to be in the same room with him.

And then there was Henry, Master-at-Arms, who always seemed to shout at his men whenever he spied James skipping on the path towards their parade grounds, his voice rising in the cadenced count till James worried Master Henry would lose his voice for good.

But where do lost voices go? James wondered. *And can they be found?* Though it was a question that plagued him for days, he found no one to ask.

Uncle Archibald, his mother's brother who lived with them ever since the Green Knight took over his castle, was the one who found James the most tiring of all. He never called James "my favorite nephew" or "my almost son," as he did with baby Bruce. Or "castle treasure," which was what he called Alexandria.

He called James "that yammering boy who never stops talking." This was ironic because Uncle Archibald was a great talker himself, and heartily disliked being interrupted when he discoursed about herbs. And he was *always* discoursing about them.

James couldn't help yammering. Couldn't

help interrupting. Couldn't help asking questions. The world seemed so big, and he knew so little about it. Surely asking questions was the best and quickest way to find out more.

Evidently, no one else felt that way.

Even Mother.

Of all the household, only Cook gave him a bit of her time.

Though his mother had banned him from the kitchen during cooking time, as he was a "distracting influence around sharp things and hot fires," he would sometimes venture in when Cook had taken a moment to put her feet up.

Whenever she saw him, she would wipe her massive hands on her apron, which, even in the early morning, would already be stained from cooking.

She'd hand him a bit of buttered white bread—well toasted over the fire—with a dollop of jam on top.

"Is it blaeberry?" he would ask. "Is it strawberry? Is it . . ." But by then his mouth would be too full to ask anything more.

Cook smiled, knowing that her trick

worked every time. She was a big woman with a smile that reminded people that once she was quite beautiful. She was thoughtful, too, and wondered why the others in the castle didn't find their own ways of distracting the young heir instead of ignoring him.

Him and his questions.

The only other person who would willingly spend time with James was Alexandria. She had adored him from the moment she'd held him in her arms, when she was ten years old.

Alexandria never shooed James away or shut her door to him. She was a very observant eighteen-year-old who read all the time—Scripture, romances, and anything on history that she could find. Best of all, she never shirked from telling him what she knew.

And as far as James was concerned, Alexandria knew *everything.*

5

In Which James Gets Alexandria to Explain Many Things

James went most often to Alexandria when he had questions, though when she was busy with young lady things—like sewing tapestries or taking lessons on the lute—he knew to stay away. And when she was off on one of her long trips, he missed her so much, he could feel an empty space in his chest.

"That's a piece of my heart gone," he would whisper to himself, though not aloud, because missing one's older sister was not a proper young duke thing to do. Besides, he didn't know if he was missing a piece from the right side of his chest or the left, and he hadn't Alexandria to tell him.

But whenever she was home and not terribly busy with young lady things, James would bombard her with questions like the names of flowers in the garden, or the songs of birds, or the seven miracles spoken of in the Hebrew Testament, or the twelve-best ways to prepare eggs. She knew all the answers. Or at least she answered where she could.

If he asked why the sky was blue or if the world was really round like the globe, or when spring would make its way to the castle again, she would lead him by the hand into their father's library to discover the books together—books on colors and books on circumnavigating the world and books that predicted weather.

"Let's see if we can find the answers here," she said, "instead of bothering every busy person in the castle."

Some of the books in the library were in English, which he *could* read, but most of the scrolls were in Latin, which he couldn't, though Alexandria translated for him.

"Girls often know Latin," she assured him.

"So do monks," he said. "And they aren't girls."

Alexandria laughed and tousled his hair. "Not even close."

She also helped him remember things by teaching him little rhymes, like:

Willie, Willie, Harry, Stee,
Harry, Dick, John, Harry three:

This was a rhyme about all the important kings up to their time. She had learned it from *her* old tutor, who no longer taught and had moved south where it was warm most of the year.

"And what about the queens?" James asked her.

Alexandria had smiled. It lit up her face, softened the angles, and meant she was extremely pleased with the question. "We shall have to figure that one out for ourselves. Make our own rhyme."

"Maybe there haven't been enough queens for a rhyme," James said.

"*Excelsior!*" Alexandria told him, which was what she said when she meant, "Well done, James."

They came up with:

Tilda, Jane, Mary, Lizzy,
They all make me very dizzy.

Then James twirled around and around, until the twirling made him fall down with actual dizziness, and Alexandria laughed at him until he joined in.

In other words, Alexandria made learning fun, something tutors never understood.

"Alexandria," he said earnestly, "I want to know the names of everything. I want to know where dogs go when they die, and who built the first Castle Callander—the one that's now only bits of crumbled walls. And why there is no dragon in our moat."

And she answered, "Dogs go to dog heaven where they course through the endless green fields. Mother says the Picts built the first Castle Callander, and Father says the Angles did. Which means they don't know. But when you are older, I bet you will find out."

"I bet I will, too," James said. And he smiled.

"As for dragons in the moat, they are long gone. Like chimera, and mermaids, and unicorns."

"Oh, I hope you're wrong about mermaids

and unicorns," said James, looking up at her with his brilliant eyes.

"I hope so, too, little brother."

James knew this was not the kind of conversation he could ever have with Cumbersome. Cumbersome just recited figures and facts in a voice so dry, it made dust scraping on the cobbles sound wet. In fact, an hour with Cumbersome and his droning voice sounded so like one of Nanny's Caldonian bagpipes that James was ready either for a nap or for a scramble with the hounds on the trail of a rabbit.

James felt bad about this view of Cumbersome, but not so bad that he didn't still call him "a dried-up stick of a man," which made Alexandria smile.

"Cumbersome," she said carefully, "is only thirty years old. Younger than Father. Or Mother."

"That can't be so," James said.

"But it is."

"Some things are simply *too* difficult to believe," James told her. "Do you want to hear a rhyme I made up about him?"

She put her fingers in her ears. "I shouldn't."

But when he started to recite it, she took her fingers out and laughed till she hiccupped.

His laugh is like Cook's grater,
His snort is like a sigh,
Yet once he was the apple
In his old dear mama's eye.
But apples all get eaten up,
And served at every course.
He so reminds me of the mush
That we call applesauce.

Alexandria stopped giggling and said, "Really, though, I know you can rhyme better than that!"

"It's how Uncle Archibald would say it," James pointed out, pinching his nose between his thumb and forefinger and pronouncing *course* in his uncle's old-fashioned, high-pitched, toffee voice so that it did, indeed, rhyme with *sauce*. And that made the two of them become convulsed again until they were limp with all the laughing.

If Cumbersome had been there to hear

them, James would have had to write a long and flowery apology to his uncle and read it aloud at the dinner table. And go without the library for a week or two.

Or even, James thought, *forever*.

But Alexandria didn't care. She dared more than James ever dreamed of. And goodness knows what she got up to when on visits to their Great-Aunt Alice, who was called "Aunt Danger" by those who knew her, and "The Duke's Odd Sister What Never Took a Husband or a Bath" by those who'd only ever heard stories about her.

Even Cumbersome mentioned her quietly when trying to make sure James didn't stray from the path of righteous study. Only he never really understood how much James truly longed for knowledge of all kinds, not just the "Right Kind." It might have made Cumbersome's stay at Castle Callander easier had he tried to understand.

But Alexandria understood. "If you tried one question at a time, James," she said, "you might get more answers."

"But I might forget the other questions,"

James protested, adding, “Why does autumn always follow summer and not winter? And why do male birds sing and not the females?”

“Let’s go to the library,” Alexandria said, taking his hand.

Even as their footsteps echoed on the marble floors, he had a final question. Looking up at her, he said, “What is the full moon full of?”

Alexandria looked at him seriously. “Green cheese,” she said.

“Really? What kind of green cheese? Is it moldy? Is it—”

She shook her head. “Joke questions get a joke answer, James.”

But James only looked confused. “I meant no joke.”

6

In Which Uncle Archibald Makes a Fateful Decision

At last, exhausted by James and his questions, Uncle Archibald told them at dinner one night that James was to be sent to Cranford Abbey to study.

"As Cranford has long lived on the charity of the Callander dukes," Uncle Archibald said, "and the Callander heirs all go to be educated there, and as your father is not here to make that decision, I am making it now."

There was a hush around the table. Even Cook, who was serving the meal, looked startled.

"But," Alexandria said to him, "usually they don't go till they turn ten or eleven."

Uncle Archibald gave her a look that should have crushed her spirit but did not. And Mother gave a clicking sound rather like a cricket in the hearth.

"James has much to learn," Uncle Archibald said slowly, as if picking his words like coins out of a jeweled box. "In case he becomes the duke sooner than expected."

Mother's hand went to her mouth as if she might pull out a single syllable of rebuke. But no sound emerged.

James was equally stunned into silence.

They all knew he meant in case the duke was dead on the road somewhere in the Holy Land.

"How . . . long?" Alexandria asked. She had a scowl on her face and her chin jutted out, like a shield ready to protect James in this battle.

"Just a little while," Archibald explained, "so we can all get some quiet, and James can learn everything he wishes. And if he does not follow their rules of silence, he will certainly be put on bread and water as a punishment."

Though "learn control" was what Uncle Archibald *actually* said, all James heard was the word *learn*, and his heart filled in the rest. Which is why he hadn't made a fuss about leaving at the table.

However, as the time came closer for him to go to Cranford, he had even more unanswered questions. Many of them to do with the unspoken words about his father.

"Why have I never seen an angel? Did Lucifer hurt anyone when he fell to earth? How do we walk about in heaven when our bones are buried below?"

Alexandria said carefully, "Those are good questions to ask the monks."

"And where do babies come from?" James asked suddenly. "And how do they get there?" Now he was thinking about his brother, Bruce, who had been annoying him that morning, wanting to play trot-trot when James wanted to read.

No one—not even Alexandria—was willing to answer that one.

Cook had mumbled something about storks, which seemed minimally possible. Nurse ventured something about the cabbage patch, which even James did not give a moment's credence to.

Alford the stableman later told Uncle Archibald that he could show James how horses were bred and born, and was almost dismissed for his impertinence, though not without a great deal of laughter on Mother's part.

James thought her laughter was tinged with sadness at the thought of him going so far away. Or at least he hoped so.

Uncle Archibald merely said in his slow way, "That's hardly necessary, Alford." And Alford was sent back to the barn without showing James anything at all.

Suddenly, it was a mere ten days before James was to leave, and he and Alexandria sat in the kitchen as the sun began to inch towards the far hills.

"I suppose," James said, "that the monks

at the monastery will teach me all that I need to know about having babies."

They were having tea, and Cook brought out honey cakes and gingerbread, as well as buns with currants and raisins. And James' favorite—slices of white bread slathered in fresh butter and covered with a mixture of cinnamon and sugar.

James and Alexandria had been reading a book together about explorations on the Continent, and without permission had taken it out of the library and had it with them. Alexandria insisted that James wipe his hands carefully, and his mouth, too, before touching the book again.

"Otherwise," she warned in a whisper, "you will be too sticky and too crumbly and will leave a mark. And then Uncle Archibald will know."

That was warning enough. James picked up the cloth and began to vigorously wipe first his hands, then his face, till the cloth was sticky all over.

She added, "It's all right to make marks on your jerkin," she said, "but not on a book. Books are sacred."

James kept wiping dutifully, this time on his jerkin, but then realized Alexandria hadn't answered his question. "But what about the monks?" he persisted. "Will they or won't they tell me where babies come from?"

"I am not certain they know anything at all about it," said Alexandria. "They do not marry and are without issue."

"What's *issue*?" he asked.

"Children." It was to be her last word on the subject, and no amount of pleading from her brother made her give any further explanation.

Even with that, James still had been very eager to go to the abbey.

Some monk will know something, he thought. *Or surely the abbot* …

But as one day followed the next, he began to worry, and after three of those days were gone, he was no longer so certain that the abbey was where he wanted to be. In fact, he feared that the abbot wouldn't warm to him or want him underfoot asking questions any more than his uncle did.

He thought, in his own way, that if no one wanted to hear his questions or answer them, he would show everyone that he could be a good and silent boy. Then maybe he wouldn't have to go to the abbey after all.

James stayed silent—or as close to silent as possible for a boy of his age and personality to manage—for about half a day. Because he was really a bit afraid and a bit sad about leaving, and yet a bit excited, too. The feelings were all wrapped together in a kind of Christmas ball that one only gets to unwind at the high table during the yuletide feast.

As he went silent, a kind of hush fell on the castle, as if it were under an enchantment, though really it was just everyone else taking a deep, cleansing breath and enjoying the cease of James' endless questions. Even Alexandria seemed to relish the quiet.

In fact, James went more than just silent. He went still. He walked slowly and quietly up the stairs, and when he came down again, he didn't slide down the banister shouting, "Yahooooo!"

He ate quickly at meals and left his dirty napkin by the side of the plate instead of forgetting and leaving it tucked in the top of his tunic to use later as a pirate's bandanna or a highwayman's mask.

He spent some of the time he had left sitting moat-side and throwing out bits of his uneaten bread to the ducks and swans who flourished there, because, as he whispered to himself, "There aren't any moat dragons here."

And as day followed day, everyone came to expect the quiet, forgetting how tiresome James had been.

But on the third day of James' silence, his mother and sister and Nanny began to worry whether in fact James had fallen ill, because since the day he'd asked his first questions at age one and a half, James had never been silent for long.

"Maybe he's got the influx," said Nanny, who fancied herself a doctor.

"Maybe he's got the heebies and the jeebies," said Alexandria, who read foreign books as well as English ones.

"Maybe he just has the grumps," his mother said. She'd had two brothers—one of them Uncle Archibald, the other in the Holy Land with her missing husband—and so she knew a bit about that sort of thing.

But just in case James *really* was ill, they made him tisanes and forced him to drink these herbal teas concocted from blessed thistles, along with oil that Cook distilled from newly caught river cod. He had to take a long soak in a warm bath, the water sprinkled lavishly with sprigs of lavender, till he smelled like a bush and had wrinkled fingers and toes.

On Uncle Archibald's command, after each warm bath, he had to run and jump into the cold Callan River, which flowed sluggishly nearby.

None of this seemed to clear up James' condition. And that night, he dreamed of his father in the faraway Holy Land. In the dream he was sure that his father—who was big and tough and sometimes funny—was never coming back home. James woke covered with sweat. He knew for certain that he didn't want to leave home. *Indeed,* he thought, *no one can give me a reason why I should.*

Leaving was three days away now, which was too big and too real to ignore. Yet it was too frightening to think about as well, which was why he thought about it every waking moment and had nightmares about it every night.

The truth was, he'd never actually been very far away from home before. When his father had first been reported missing, James—as the possible new duke and Lord of Callanshire—had been protected.

"Overprotected," Uncle Archibald had grumbled. "The treasury cannot stand the extra pay." He meant he'd have to cut back on the herb garden.

That was how it came about that James never got to leave the shire, except to go riding in the castle woods with guards or fish its many streams. He'd never gone anywhere for a weekend, nor anywhere overnight.

It seemed so unfair. Alexandria got to spend weeks at Aunt Alice's house in Hockney, studying tapestry making, of all things. Aunt Alice was noted for her needlework and her oddities. It was said she drank mead and could shoot a great bow like a man. She could read seven languages and speak the language of Cathay. (Though not read it.) But she was also the best tapestry maker in the three counties of Callanshire: Callan, East Riding, and Hockney.

Aunt Alice was supposed to instruct Alexandria on the fine art of womanly pursuits if she was ever to get married.

Even baby Bruce, once he was three and it was certain he would live, would get to go on a fortnight trip in the summer with Mother to visit the grandparents two shires away.

But ever since his father had gone missing, James had to stay at home. Never to travel, never to go outside the castle grounds. Never, that was, until now. With Bruce now a healthy two-year-old, and James so full of questions, even Mother was ready to let him go. In fact, she was eager to see the last of him.

Or so it seemed to James.

He woke in the middle of the night before his ninth birthday sobbing about a stomachache. And it was true. His stomach hurt, or maybe it was his head. Or even—he thought—his heart.

Nanny woke Mother.

"Will they even like me at the abbey?" James asked as his mother bent over him, spooning warm milk with honey into his mouth.

She ran a hand though his shining golden hair, so like her own. "How could they not?" she said.

"I'm tiresome," he whispered. "Everyone says so."

But at that very minute, Bruce in the

other bed sat up talking in his sleep as he often did, and Mother turned towards him, so she didn't actually hear what James had just said, and therefore didn't contradict him.

Suddenly, the honey milk threatened to come up again. James reached for the bowl on his bed stand.

But when his mother put her hand on his head again, the milk settled down and so did James. And soon, with his mother singing him his old nursery lullaby and rubbing his head with lavender cream, he went back to sleep.

7

In Which James Finally Gets to Leave the Castle

"Will the monks answer my questions?" James asked Cumbersome the next morning. The honeyed milk had done its work. Or else a good night's sleep had. He had forgotten all about his birthday in the relief of being well again.

"To the best of their ability, I'm certain," the tutor replied, nodding his head, which, James sometimes thought, looked very much like one of Uncle Archibald's allium flowers waving on a single leggy stalk. He handed a small book to James with a blue ribbon around it. "Suitable for your ninth birthday, m'lord," he said.

James took a quick peek at the spine of the book. *A Boy's Book of Small Prayers.* He wished it had been a book that identified beetles or talked about globes, but he knew better than to complain. "I am honored," he said.

Later that morning, James went and sat in the garden, where he practiced the rhymes Alexandria had taught him, the ones about the kings and queens, then one about the seven seas, and another about the twelve tribes of Israel, until he was word perfect. He knew he would need to be word perfect for the monks to appreciate him.

He'd have liked to ask Alexandria if he was saying them correctly, but she was off with Aunt Alice for her own lessons, so she was not around for him to ask anything of her at all.

So he decided to go to his mother's rooms, where he guessed she'd be sitting with her ladies, perhaps unpicking a section of a very large tapestry of soldiers hunting a unicorn that she'd been working on ever since he could remember.

James knew unicorns could be very vicious beasts and their horns were greatly prized by kings, but he rather liked the beasts.

Alexandria had read him a treatise on unicorns. She had a rhyme for that as well.

The unicorn's a wily beast.
Its horn is six foot long at least.
Which could quite cut a man in two
If that is what the beast would do.
Its feet are cloven like a deer,
But no fair maiden need have fear,
For if she sits and does not stir,
The unicorn will come to her.

He went up to his mother's rooms quietly, and if she had held out her hand to him, he wouldn't have said a word. But she was busy and hardly turned to look at him. So in a torrent of words like a cloudburst, all the questions he hadn't asked for days and days seemed to tumble out.

"But what if I don't want to go to the

abbey? What if it makes me have more stomachaches? What if no one knows to give me honeyed milk? What if—"

Mother looked up sternly. "We Callanders have always done our duty," she said. "And going to the abbey is yours, James." Then she reached down at her feet and drew up a wrapped box and handed it to him. "For your ninth birthday, my son. I wish your sister were here to share a cake with you. Cook has made one special. Now remember what I said about doing your duty."

"Will the monks treat me well?" he asked his uncle in his study, where he was scribbling his name at the bottom of some great document and looking peeved.

"They had better," Uncle Archibald said. "Your late father and I are much too important to the abbey's finances for them to treat you poorly. I trust they will appreciate your finer qualities. Your ... your ..." And here Uncle Archibald thought a bit, then said, "Your love of learning, for one. And your curious mind."

James ignored the word *late*. His father was never late for anything.

"Do you mean," James asked, "that my curiosity is odd, or that my mind is strange?"

"I said what I meant," his uncle told him. "Now run along. I have business to attend to."

At the door, James turned. "It's my birthday," he said.

Without looking up from the paper he was reading, Uncle Archibald said, "So it is. Celebrate it with care."

James went downstairs to the kitchen, where Cook had a birthday cake all baked, and they shared it without questions, without answers. Because cake is like a stopper in a bottle. It keeps things corked up inside.

The day James was to travel to Cranford Abbey dawned a pearly grey, which fitted his mood. He sat up in bed and stared out the corbelled window.

"Good!" he said to the maid, a plain young woman aptly named Jane, who'd come in to open all the curtains and bring him a basin of hot water for his wash. "It's all good."

"Good, young sir?" Jane asked.

"Good that the day is as sorry looking as I feel." He dangled his feet over the side of the bed.

"One day, I suppose," he said to himself, but loud enough that Jane the maid could hear him, "I will be old enough and tall enough so that when I put my feet over the bed, they will touch the rushes on the floor. Isn't that so?"

"You don't want to be rushing time," Jane told him. "All too soon you'll have to work for your supper."

He thought about that a moment, then said, "But I'm a duke's son." *And maybe even already the duke*, he said to himself, but didn't want to think any more about it.

She stared at him, her hands on her hips. "And doesn't your uncle work hard to keep this castle and all the people in it fed and safe?"

James had never thought of it like that before. Yes, the Callanders did their duty, but that meant things like keeping up a fine appearance and saying please and thank you and learning their ABCs. And sometimes—as his father had done—following the king into a just war. But he never considered keeping people fed and safe as important work. Maybe it was what made Uncle Archibald so cranky.

Then he had a further thought. *Learning is work, too.*

And so was being a hero like his father, he supposed. He grimly thought that his father had done his duty even though he may have died for it and been buried in a foreign land.

"Do you think I'll be able to work for my supper when I'm grown?" He meant learning and being a hero more than he meant keeping people fed and safe, though Jane was not to know that.

Jane nodded. "We little folk count on it."

"You're not so little," he pointed out. She was a big girl. Tall, too.

"And you're not so grown," she retorted,

"that I can't report your cheek to your uncle." But she smiled when she said it, and was still smiling when she left the room moments later, so he knew she wouldn't.

James had lots of things to think about as he got dressed in the clothes that Nanny had set out the night before. Questions about growing and taking care of the little folk and being a hero so filled his mind that he forgot for the moment to be sad.

Nanny came in to help with the last bit of packing and the clean clothes she was sending along to the abbey because—as she had said to James' mother only that morning—"No abbot is going to say we sent a duke's son there with greying clothes and a smudge on his nose."

His mother had sighed before telling her, "I'm afraid that once he's gone off with the guard, the smudge is inevitable."

As Nanny set down the clothes on the newly vacated bed, she took out the soft, wet clootie and headed in James' direction.

"I'm glad of one thing, Nanny," James said, in between the swishes of the clootie across his face.

"What's that?" Nanny asked, too distracted to see she'd stepped into a trap.

"No more wet face cloths," James said. "No one cares if a boy has a smudge at an abbey."

He thought he was being sassy and clever, but in that he was quite wrong, for he was soon to find out what the abbot thought of smudges. And Nanny, who had known him since he was a newborn, simply ignored him and scrubbed all the harder until he could feel the shine as hot spots on his cheeks and nose and behind each ear.

Alexandria had not come home from Aunt Danger's house but had sent a note by a fast rider, along with a birthday package. It turned out to be a sheaf of foolscap paper she had bound herself and decorated with Latin mottoes, plus a goose-feather pen and a precious bottle of ink so black it looked the color of one of Nanny's famous peaty lochs. Or at least the color as she described it.

"So you can write your questions down without troubling too many people," Alexandria's note said. "And learn Latin at the same time. I shall be home in fifteen days."

Though, of course, James knew he would be long gone by then.

The first page said *Fiat lux. Let there be Light.*

The illumination Alexandria had done was of a great shaft of golden light shooting down between two clouds onto the head of a boy with white-gold hair and a smudge on his nose.

"That's me," James said, scarcely breathing. He packed the precious sheaf of papers between his tunics in the bag.

But Nanny took the pen and ink away because, as she said, "It will get all over your freshly laundered clothes. Besides, if there is one thing abbeys have a lot of, it's pens. And as for ink, they drink it, I hear."

Even James did not believe her.

The men-at-arms, six of them, were already outside and standing at attention when

James got downstairs. He could see them through the open door.

"Breakfast first," Mother said.

He only toyed with his food, pushing the fresh hen's eggs from one side of the plate to the other till they were all scrumbled around just the way he liked them.

"Not hungry," he mumbled.

"Nonsense," Uncle Archibald said. "You need sustenance for the trip." But in this he was mistaken.

James joined the men-at-arms soon after, with nothing in his stomach, but he carried a small satchel of food packed by Cook just in case. He wasn't sure what case that would be. But he carried the satchel with him to his horse.

Horse, of course, was too elevated a name for the size of it. Horse was what you called Alexandria's great white gelding. Horse was what you called the master-at-arms' brown destrier or the men-at-arms' coursers. But James' horse was a Moors pony, named Run-well, who was trained for long travels. It was James' favorite of all the ponies in the stable.

Runwell loved to nuzzle apples out of James' hand, and there were plenty of apples to be had. Castle Callander had a lovely orchard.

James had been careful the evening before to gather a few of the small young, hard apples, the kind the pony liked best. They were hidden between the extra shirts and hose that Nanny had packed, though she hadn't noticed.

Or if she had, she hadn't said.

Once James had been lifted onto Runwell, Master Henry, the master-at-arms, called out, "Mount up!" in his grumble of a voice, and as one the six men swung onto their own horses.

James turned around once and saw Nanny holding a waving baby Bruce. The maids and Cook were standing behind, under the portcullis. And to the other side, almost as if she did not want to be seen, was Mother. She seemed to be weeping.

He wondered why.

8

THE FIRST REAL REPORT OF JAMES' ADVENTURE

The trip wasn't supposed to be difficult. It was only fifty miles, a mere three days and two nights. In fact, Uncle Archibald called it "straight as a bow shot."

It was anything but.

That first day they were shadowed by a pack of wolves, grey as mist, who seemed to fade in and out of the woody paths.

Runwell was all nerves by the time the wolves were sighted, and twice had threatened to run away with James, even though James had held him expertly with the reins.

The troop stopped for a minute, and three of the men-at-arms fired arrows towards the pack, which served to hold them off, though no wolves were actually hit.

James was happy. Runwell even more so.

But James was less happy when, a few minutes later, James was told to dismount. It was said politely but firmly by the burly sergeant who handed him up with little ceremony to ride pillion behind Master Henry.

As if I'm some fair lady needing rescue, James thought. But he was smart enough not to let Master Henry or the men know his thoughts.

"Nothing to fear from the wolves," Master Henry said brightly, turning around in the saddle. "It's winter, when food is scarce, that wolves are a pestilence. And here it's midsummer."

"Then why take me off Runwell?" James asked.

"Because your pony has become too skittish and unpredictable," Master Henry said in a voice that was much too jolly for the occasion.

Grown-ups, James thought, *often sound that way when they really mean just the opposite*.

"I thought I was handling him well," James said, not letting too much of his disappointment show. "Callanders do their duty, and riding the pony was mine."

"Keeping Callanders safe is *my* duty," Master Henry replied. "Especially the heir." He didn't mention that James was possibly already the duke.

James had never thought of it that way—that Master Henry's duty might trump his own.

"And I wouldn't like to be the one to have to tell her ladyship that I lost her son. Or her son's horse."

James wondered if Master Henry knew Jane the maid, but thought better than to mention it. Instead he said, "What will happen to the pony?"

"Last man-of-arms will tie the pony's reins to his own. You will need the pony whole and hale at the abbey."

After a night sleeping by the fire in the forest, James slept in a tent by himself—which somehow made him more rather than less worried about wolves. But they saw no more of the pack.

However, this didn't mean they were trouble-free. The next morning, they came upon a great elk with horns that seemed to reach the sky. The elk chased them away from the meadow they'd meant to cross, for he was guarding his harem of cows.

"We will go along to another crossing," Master Henry said steadily. "No need to tussle with an elk in season unless we mean to pack the meat with us. And we do not have time to slaughter and dress it for travel. Nor can I spare the men to cart the meat home to Castle Callander."

"You could give it to the abbey," James said.

"Your mother is already giving the abbey its greatest gift," Master Henry replied.

"She is?" James tried to puzzle out what that might be.

"You," said Master Henry. "And she's wept many a night with that decision."

James could scarcely credit it. *I didn't think Mother even liked me, with all my tiresome questions. Not now that she has Bruce, who is no trouble at all.* But he was careful to keep that thought to himself, too. In fact, he was keeping rather a lot of thoughts to himself now that he didn't have Alexandria to talk to.

They spent the next night in the forest as well, and though James volunteered to stand guard with one of the men-at-arms, he was told in no uncertain terms that he was not to be foolish.

"You are our lord's oldest son, and you need to be well rested for the remainder of the trip," Master Henry told him, a bead of sweat making a path down the side of his face, just in front of his right ear.

James puzzled about this for a moment, but before he could ask outright, Master Henry continued. "Besides, Nanny would kill me if I let you get dirty from guard duty. And your mother would have my heart served up to the hounds if I kept you from your sleep."

Before it was truly dark, Master Henry escorted James to his single tent pitched next to the fire as if he were a child still in the nursery. James thought the elk—should it wander into their camp—would make quick work of the tent. Wild boar and a bear would be as quick to destroy it. But suddenly he was too tired to complain.

Besides, the men-at-arms would take turns watching the perimeter. Perhaps they would shoot the elk anyway. He knew they were all excellent bowmen. And an elk was too big a target to miss. He knew he was safe.

Master Henry turned and walked over to his men, but a tiny bit of their conversation drifted back to James as he lay half awake on his small camp bed.

"The good Lord save me from nine-year-olds," Master Henry said. "Luckily, I was away at war with the last duke when my twins were that age."

A small thread of laughter made its way through the men, tying them together in a knot.

James felt unhappy to be both dismissed

and laughed at. But even more, he was saddened at the thought that his own father—the last duke—had been away from him when James was even younger than Master Henry's twins. And he'd never returned. That sadness suddenly overwhelmed him as he thought of his father, a tall man with a great golden moustache and a ready laugh.

James was suddenly wide awake.

Sorrow, he thought, a bit dramatically, *can do that.*

He was determined to stay awake.

When the moon was half obscured by a cloud, so no one could see him, he slipped out through the back flap of the tent, and suddenly saw a mist of white between the trees.

For a moment, he worried it might be the wolves returning. But the mist was too high off the ground for them. Then he worried about the elk and its females. *Elk*, Alexandria had once told him, *are not predictable creatures.*

But elk were dark, not light-colored animals. So the white mist could not be them.

Then he wondered if he was seeing a fairy

raid, which was when the fey folk rode out on their white horses. There were ballads about that. They were supposed to have bells on their saddles and reins, and he'd heard nothing that sounded like bells.

Or perhaps, he thought, *it's the Wild Hunt headed by Herne the Hunter, who goes racing through the forest hunting down the souls of the damned, the Hounds of Hell baying at his horse's feet.* But just as there were no sounds of bells ringing, there was no sound of hounds. Just the huffing of the horses who were hobbled for the night, the warbling of night birds, and a single owl calling to a prospective mate.

He peered silently into the white mist but could not make out what he was seeing. So he went back into the tent, lay down on the bed, and closed his eyes.

After two more days in the saddle, James' arms had grown tired of holding on to Master Henry's armor, and his bottom was sore from riding all day. There'd been no more encounters with beasts or phantoms.

James had learned one thing, and one thing only. Travel took a long time.

And it was not as comfortable as being at home.

By the time they got within sight of the abbey, looking down where it nestled in the bowl of a valley, surrounded by cultivated fields and orchards, James had been allowed back on Runwell.

It made both James and the pony happy.

And so by late afternoon, they arrived, with James riding secure at the very front of the little troop, suddenly feeling very grown up. He *was* grown up, he thought, because he'd ridden a long way and now knew what it was like to travel.

And because he was en route to a place where he could ask questions of people who would have answers for him.

And because he was a Callander, and his father's son.

They rounded the last switchback on the trail, and the gates of the abbey opened to him like a father's welcoming arms.

9

In Which James Is Homesick and Alone

Now, the afternoon James arrived at the abbey was a week before the last of the heroes had attempted getting rid of the unicorns. But as a new arrival, he wasn't much considered, even though he was the local duke's son, because everyone's attention was on the wily beasts in the orchard.

In fact, the master-of-arms had been more welcomed than James.

Abbot Aelian greeted the troop with a broad smile and took Master Henry aside, ignoring James.

"We have a small problem," the abbot whispered, and pointed to the orchard.

James was turned over to a round man, shaped rather like a barrel of wine and who had a badly shaved round spot in the middle of his head, called a tonsure, which looked like the lawn at Castle Callander after a long winter—stubbly and a brownish-grey. The monk took James' satchel in hand and led him into a low stone house and along a straight corridor with doors opening on either side, his sandals hardly making a sound on the stone floor.

James followed dutifully behind. Indeed, what else could he do? As they went along, he asked, "What is this place?"

"The dortoir, where the lads stay."

"Are there many?"

"Ten of them, mostly oblates."

"What's an oblate?" It sounded strange to James.

"Boys given by their parents as gifts to the abbey to be raised by us and to honor the Lord."

"Am I an oblate?"

"For certain, you are a gift. But not an oblate, for you shall return home when called to become duke if God wills it early, or on your fifteenth birthday."

"And when will I meet the abbot?"

The round monk turned to James. "We dinna speak in the halls, lad. Though we are nae a totally silent order, we practice quiet in our daily lives."

"But . . ."

"Nae buts."

James shivered. It wasn't that the dortoir halls were particularly cold or damp. But still he shivered. Perhaps the other boys would answer his questions. He wondered what they'd be like.

He'd never had much to do with other boys, that is, except for his brother, Bruce, who was still a baby, and the gardener's sons, who were older than him. And besides, they all worked.

As he was contemplating the long hallway and wondering which might be his room, the monk stopped before a doorway and opened it. Inside there was a small cot on a wooden base, a mattress stuffed with straw, and a thin blanket at the bedfoot. At the bed's head was a wooden table on which stood a candle, a prayer book, and a mug for water. On the bed were a rough brown tunic that had a brown cord to tie around the waist, a heavy brown cloak, and a pair of brown hose.

"But I have my own clothes," James said to the monk, pointing to his satchel.

"We've nae frills here," the monk said. Though as he was rather round, James assumed he meant in clothing but not in food. "However, as the duke's son, you will be allowed to keep the bag here with you. Now climb into your oblate clothes, and I will wait out in the hall while you do."

Dutifully, James got into the brown clothes, but the tunic itched around the neck, and the cord was much too long, so he had to knot it three times. The cloak was badly sewn and too bulky over his thin shoulders. Patches covered the hose.

All at once, James was incredibly aware that he was far from home. He suddenly missed everyone in the castle, even Cumbersome, with his dry voice. Even Uncle Archibald and his disdain.

James was aware that his eyes were filling up, and he pressed his fist in his right eye to keep from weeping, but he must have let out a little cry, because the round monk came in shaking his head. “Tha poor lad, never far from home before, I wager.”

At this, James burst into tears, and the monk patted him clumsily on the back, saying, “Better to get it out now, lad, before the others come in from their chores. Tha dinna want to be seen as a sniveling bairn.”

James recognized this as Geordie talk for a weeping baby, as one of his tutors had been a Geordie. He used the sleeve of the tunic to wipe his tears away. Then he smiled up at the monk. “I'm James,” he said.

“Oh, we all know about thee,” the round monk said. “But thee will have a time learning all of us. So best start here.”

“*Fiat lux*,” said James, remembering the first page of the illuminated notes Alexandria had sent.

“Ah, a Latin scholar!” said the monk.

"That's excellent. I am Brother Luke, Master of Illuminations."

James did not bother to set him right about the Latin. Just grinned and asked, "What does a master of illuminations do?"

"Why, I make pictures to bring color and light to the Word of God," said Brother Luke. "And now let us go to dinner." He patted his belly. "I'm starved."

James followed Brother Luke in silence down the hallway, though in his head were still many questions. And the greatest of these was whether he would be allowed to say good-bye to Master Henry and the men, the only people at the abbey who knew anything about him at all.

But Master Henry's men had been asked to help the monks defend the orchard. The men-at-arms had fired off their arrows, some even hitting their marks, and the unicorns had chased them up the trees, where the six men and Master Henry spent a miserable dusk to dinnertime up in the branches of the golden apple trees.

As soon as the sun set and the unicorns

departed, their bellies full of apples, Master Henry had gathered his defeated troops and left the abbey for home, not even stopping in the dining hall for a meal that the cook had made especially for them.

It was clear that Master Henry was less frightened of the duchess's wrath than he was of another encounter with the unicorns.

He left James in the abbey without a farewell.

And since the other boys were yet to come back from their chores, James ate in silence with Brother Luke and then was escorted by the monk to his room.

"Tha will get the lay of the land soon enough," Brother Luke said. "And I'll no walk ye back again, as it will make you the mock of the boys if I do."

James nodded and went into his small room, which was less than a quarter of the size of the bedroom in Castle Callander. He lay down in the narrow cot, thinking he would never get sleep. But no sooner did he blow out the candle and close his eyes than he began to dream.

In his dream, his father came riding down

the path to the abbey on a white unicorn, and when he reached the abbey door, James was waiting for him. His father bent down and gathered him up in his arms, laughing.

"Good to be home," his dream father said. "Good to have you in my arms again, my favorite lad."

James slept so soundly on the narrow cot that he didn't even hear the boys coming to bed in the rooms next to his. But he met them in the morning, a rough-and-tumbling crew of ten, who were only a bit curious about him and rather more interested in what had happened when the men-at-arms had fired off their arrows.

One of the cook boys said, "I heard they hit the mark with three of the beasts. Right here." And he pointed to his chest.

"And what happened next?" asked a red-headed boy who seemed to James to be the leader of the pack.

"They neither fell nor bled, but limped away," said the cook boy. "Brother Luke said that their horns are magical, and one—the big stallion—put his horn on the spot where the unicorns were hit and, as he watched, the wound healed."

James sat there stunned into silence. He looked down at the breakfast. There was porridge and a coarse brown bread, but no eggs or meats or fruit, even though the monks had a fine orchard and a long row of gardens. He had seen them as he and the Callander men-at-arms had ridden in.

He sighed.

The boys all turned to him.

"So who be you?" asked the redheaded boy.

"James Callander," James replied.

"I'm Bartholomew," the boy said. "I wager you're the duke's son."

James nodded and almost smiled before Bartholomew's next words.

"You're not the leader of us," he said.

James was glad that he hadn't held out his hand or said more than those few words. He just concentrated on the meal, or what there was of it. He didn't like the brown bread or the rough, seedy jams. He missed Cook's honey cakes and gingerbread. In fact, he missed Cook herself.

And then there were the prayers. At every tolling of the bell, day and night, the priest, the monks, the abbot, and the boys had to pray. He had never prayed so much in his life with so little to pray about. Except praying to see his father again. And his home.

To make matters worse, no one had the time or the energy or the will to answer his questions, because everyone—from the abbot down to the young oblate—was concerned about the golden apples.

The golden apples and the unicorns.

So James was miserable. And cold. And lonely.

He was homesick. And heartsick. And hungry.

10

In Which James Is Up a Tree

The monks were not unkind to James; they just treated him as if he wasn't there. Once they learned he had his alphabet and could already read—and that he could write, too, though badly—he was turned over to Brother Luke.

Brother Luke was the one who had taken him to his room that first day. He was soft-spoken and had a passion for italics.

"What is italics?" asked James, hoping it was something good to eat.

"It is a slant of the pen, a curl like an ocean

wave," Luke told him in that soft voice. "It is the best style in which to write the words of God."

James, who had read the latest of Alexandria's Latin mottoes just that morning, responded, "*Semper paratus*," which made Brother Luke smile.

"If you are indeed *semper paratus*—always ready—then let us begin."

He showed James to a high desk with an inkwell and a goose-feather pen. "Write semper paratus," he told James.

With quite a bit of blots and splots and three tries at spelling *paratus*, James did as told. Then, on a whim, he made a squiggle that looked something like a horse's head on the right side, with a spiral horn. The horn, at least, looked real.

Brother Luke nodded. "A good first try. Now this is what it would look like in italics." His hand held the pen steady and began to sweep the pen across the page. To James' astonishment, the pen left not a spot or a blot. The ink flowed across the scroll like a river in flood, with waves capped by little curlicues.

"Oh!" James said. It was quite the most beautiful writing he'd ever seen.

And when Brother Luke swiftly added three or four lines, a little unicorn head of his own with its eyes black and shining, James thought he could almost see the beast's breath floating on the page.

"Will I ever be able to write like that?" he asked.

"All it takes is a steady hand, a heart to God, and practice, practice, practice," Brother Luke said.

James put his hand over his heart. "*Semper paratus*," he whispered.

Brother Luke seemed pleased at how quickly James learned, though he didn't overpraise him. All he ever said was "*Commodus*" in a low, even voice, meaning, "A good standard."

Alexandria would have cried out, "Excelsior!" when James wrote out his first alphabet by himself. And when James finished that first week's long task, he himself cried out, "Excelsior!"

Brother Daffyd, two desks away in the scriptorium, only shook his head slightly and muttered, "Excess of emotion and vanity is to be avoided."

But Brother Luke just smiled at James. "What motto have you today?"

James tried to remember, but it was a fragment that seemed to be floating out of reach. Then, as he put his pen down carefully, he had it. *Labor omnia vincit.* Alexandria had sketched a pitchfork stuck upright in a mound of dirt to illuminate it.

"Labor conquers all. That's a good one," Brother Luke said.

But all was not just scripting and learning the italic hand. During the fortnight that the unicorns were off digesting and excreting, the monks were busy plotting traps for them.

There was a meeting one evening of everyone in the abbey—and that included the cook and the potboys as well—in which Brother Daffyd showed a chart with three different kinds of traps on it. One was for catching a unicorn by the foot, using a rope and a knot that grew tighter the more a beast struggled.

One was made of forged steel that had a set of steel teeth, so when a unicorn even so much as brushed by it, the trap snapped at its heels and held tight.

Sitting with the ten boys at the meeting, right behind the redhead who was in the pew in front of him, James overheard him whisper, “I wager that will break a few bones!”

The boys murmured with excitement, and even James got caught up in their fervor.

The third trap involved digging ditches but, as the abbot pointed out, it could damage the trees themselves and so was without merit.

The next morning in the scriptorium, James said suddenly to Brother Luke, “Won’t I be needed to help in the unicorn battle? What is making letters compared to that?”

He was thinking of the traps, of course, and the excitement that had coursed through the boys as Brother Daffyd had explained how to build them and how they worked.

Brother Luke’s usually smiling face turned

serious. The twinkle in his eye was gone. "We were not set down on this earth to fight unicorns but to make peace with all that lives. You and I will work on your handwriting. If the others wish to work on traps, they will answer for it in heaven."

James thought that making traps might actually be more fun, and maybe make the boys like him, but he didn't want to say so. He liked Brother Luke and did not want to disappoint him. So he nodded and settled down to work, because once his mind and hand were on the curls and whorls of the letters, he wasn't thinking of unicorns or of home.

Every once in a while he'd look up from the smudges on the practice scroll and wipe his hand across his cheek. He didn't even know he had made the gesture.

And each time, Brother Luke wiped the ink mark on James' cheek with the sleeve of his robe, just as Nanny had done when James had smudged himself.

"Thank you," James muttered. "Thank you."

"*Nehil est,*" Brother Luke would respond,

meaning—so James discovered—"It is no problem."

That night, instead of saying the evening prayers as the other boys were doing, down on their knees by their hard beds with the thin blankets, James whispered to himself:

Willie, Willie, Harry, Stee,
Harry, Dick, John, Harry three . . .

If he'd thought it would make him any less homesick, he was wrong, because it brought back Alexandria even more clearly. Misery, large and tasseled, hung over his shoulders like a Hebrew shawl.

The next morning, without actually counting which day it was, he went outside by himself before dawn and climbed up a green Plainsong tree that stood on the edge of the first line of golden Hosannahs. He found the perfect protruding limb, and as the sun rose over the orchard, he looked west, his back to the rising sun, gazing longingly in the direction of home.

With the red sky behind him and the shadows of the trees stretching before him, he felt—for the first time since coming to the abbey—a kind of peace.

And then he heard a sound behind him. Startled, he turned, expecting it to be Brother Luke scolding him for missing prayers. Instead it was a straggle of unicorns, not a herd but a few outliers who had not had their fill of the apples. They came trotting almost silently through the orchard and were coming his way. They were like a white mist threading through the trees.

He remembered seeing that mist on his way to the abbey, thinking it was wolves or the fairy raid or Herne the Hunter and the Wild Hunt.

Excelsior! he thought.

Just then he heard another sound, a high, piercing whistle.

James looked for the sound and saw it was the redheaded boy, Bartholomew, with another boy riding pillion, coming through the Plainsong trees. The horse they were riding was Runwell, and Bartholomew was sawing away at the reins while the other boy was simultaneously kicking the poor pony forward. That was not the way to ride Runwell, who was a sweet creature, and James was furious. He was just about to shout out to them to get off his horse when he saw they were accompanied by a knight in green armor with a helmet sporting a bright green feather. The green hero's hunting hawk flew above, soaring through the lightening sky with its great wings. There were three brindle hounds by the knight's side, two on the left and one on the right.

The knight's whistle, meant for the hounds, had alerted the unicorns, who lifted their heads as one. He laughed and rode right under the limb where James perched. It was to be the last time the knight laughed at the white creatures.

As the knight lifted his lance ready for a throw, the two boys on Runwell charged the unicorns from behind, herding them forward toward the waiting knight.

The knight carried a huge quiver of arrows over his shoulder, and his bow lay across his lap—one of those longbows that had just come into Callanshire for the first time the year before. However, instead of showering the unicorns with the arrows, he stood in his stirrups and aimed at the lead unicorn, a scrawny creature with one gold eye and one brown eye.

But before the lance left his hand, a unicorn stallion, with a toss of its head and long white mane dancing in the wind, struck the warhorse from behind, dislodging the green knight.

The would-be hero tumbled into the grass, lost his lance, lost his helmet, lost his bow and arrows, lost his temper, and almost lost his right leg.

He backed away, eyeing the trees, but seemingly realized he was too heavily armored to climb. But not—it turned out—too heavily armored to run.

Run he did, back the way he'd come, his dogs and horse running with him, the hawk screaming above them as they ran. Once he'd retreated well into the green apple territory, the unicorns lost interest in him, the stallion disappeared back into the thicket of apple trees, and the younger, smaller unicorns turned to finish off Runwell.

Bartholomew and the other boy slid down the pony on opposite sides and began to run in two different directions as James took action.

Without thinking it through, he leaped down from the tree, tearing his cloak as he did, and landed on the back of the scrawny unicorn, shouting as he did so, "Not my pony, you horned imp of Satan! Not my Runwell!" His voice rose in pitch till he was screaming like a pig in labor.

The knight didn't notice James leaping from the tree. He didn't seem to notice anything but the path of his retreat. And he was making so much clanking and huffing noises as he ran, he didn't hear anything either.

But Bartholomew did. When he realized the unicorns were not chasing him, he stopped and turned. Hands on hips, he watched as James seemed to bewitch the small troop of unicorns with his passionate cry.

Once the unicorns had stopped, James managed to get himself atop Runwell and race off towards the abbey. If he saw the knight, Bartholomew, or the other boy, he did not stop for them. All he wanted to do was to make sure his pony was safe and in its stall again.

Once out of the orchard and on his way to the mews where the horses were kept, James smiled. *I will write and tell Alexandria all about this adventure,* he thought, *if Brother Luke will allow me a piece of paper and a pen.*

By the time he'd gotten Runwell settled, rubbed down, and fed, James was hungry enough to eat anything put before him.

He found everyone atwitter at his morning-long absence from studies and prayer. And the boys—especially Bartholomew—proclaimed him the one true hero of the day.

11

In Which James Forms a Plan

Before James could eat anything, he was summoned to the scriptorium by a monk whose name he didn't know, a short man, hardly out of his boyhood, James guessed.

So he ran off to the other end of the dortoir, where the scriptorium was housed. When he entered, Brother Luke looked up, pen in hand, disappointment clearly etched on his face. He shook his head at James and said, "*Tibi non licet.*" That was not allowed.

James stared down at his feet for a minute, trying to look reasonably contrite before asking about the paper and pen for the letter to Alexandria.

For the first time, Brother Luke snapped at him. "They are too precious for such trivial pursuits," he said.

"But . . ." James began. It was not a good start to a convincing argument.

Brother Luke added, "You have been ordered—not invited—to the abbot's palace to explain yourself, and I am to bring you."

The abbot has a palace? James had seen no palace on the abbey grounds. Nothing tall and turreted like Castle Callander or even a tower house like Battenberg, where his mother had been born and raised. There was a tapestry at Castle Callander she had done by memory when she was first a bride at the castle.

"Come with me." Brother Luke turned, and James was forced to follow without eating anything at all. He wasn't afraid, just hungry.

Quickly, they walked down the shadowy corridor and out of the low, blocky building that looked more like a stable than a house for monks and boys.

For all that he was a round man, used to sitting long hours in the scriptorium, Brother Luke could move at a fast pace when he needed to. They were soon at the abbot's palace, which was—in James' considered opinion—not a palace at all, just a two-story building with whitewash on the outer walls. Inside he found it decorated with several awkward tapestries of the Crucifixion and the Annunciation.

The little James knew about tapestries came from watching his mother work on them. Still, to his untutored eye, these old, unraveling wall hangings were nowhere near as well sewn as hers, or as pretty.

Castle Callander is much handsomer in every way, he thought, and another wave of homesickness washed over him like a tide.

Brother Luke left James at the abbot's study door. And only now did James have the time to wonder why he'd been called to see the abbot who had—rather steadfastly—not asked for him in all the days he had been at the abbey. Odd indeed, since James was the son and heir of the duke, the abbey's greatest benefactor.

Was it, James thought, just about his spying on the unicorns, or was it more about skipping his lessons? *Or does it have to do with challenging the other boys who took my pony without asking?* He feared he would be put on bread and water for breaking a rule. *Though*, he thought ruefully, *at least it will be some food*.

He knocked a little tentatively on the study door and, when no one answered, knocked louder.

Brother Joseph opened the door and looked down at James without a word, his long face made longer by the silence. He led James into the study, where Abbot Aelian sat by the fire.

"You," the abbot began without preamble, "have a duty to your mother and to me, and putting yourself in danger is not part of my agreement with her."

"What agreement is that, sir?" James blurted out, suddenly blushing at his own boldness.

The abbot didn't answer immediately, but the fire snapped out a hot rejoinder.

At last Abbot Aelian, in his careful way,

said, "To educate you, to teach you Latin, Hebrew, Greek, and the Scriptures. To show you how to write a good hand. To lead you into an understanding of the world. And ..." The abbot hesitated.

James held his breath, wondering if it was his turn to speak. He waited some more.

But the abbot seemed to be finished.

"Sir," James said, trying to shift the subject, desperately thinking what to say, and then blurting out the first thing that came to mind: "What is the full moon full of?"

The abbot smiled as if he was unused to doing any such thing. "Not green cheese."

James relaxed. He smiled back then—his face reddening with the effort of speaking to such an imposing person. "Sir, can I ..." He took a deep breath and then said the very last thing he should have said. "Can I help?"

"With the full moon?"

It took a moment for James to realize the abbot was teasing him, since the man's face had returned to its usual dour expression, the thin lips clamped shut.

"Oh, no, sir." James felt his tongue was

suddenly too large for his mouth. This had never happened before, certainly not at home, where he just said anything he wanted to. He bit his lip and—oddly—the pain of it gave him courage to speak further. "I mean help with the unicorns. I watched them closely, you know. For the *whole* of today." He knew it was a bit of an exaggeration, but the abbot wouldn't know that.

"A *whole* day?"

James knew he couldn't repeat the exaggeration. He wondered what he could possibly say next, but Abbot Aelian went on as if ignoring James' confusion. He raised his left point finger and said, "We have been watching the unicorns for a whole three years, my son. Though perhaps not from your vantage point."

James could feel his face get cold and then hot. He stuttered. What came out were not words exactly but sounds: "Ahhh, ummm . . ."

As if Abbot Aelian had suddenly become sensitive to James' distress, he added, "If the heroes cannot help us, James, I do not see how you can."

The abbot's fingers trembled as if he, and not James, was nervous.

Just then James had an idea. It came out of nowhere, and yet even as he said it, he knew that—if it worked—it could solve many problems at once.

"There is," James began, "one hero who has not come to the abbey's aid yet."

The abbot looked shocked, or at least he gave James that impression. "I am certain I have given dinner to every hero within the seven kingdoms and more besides." His voice was dry—not dry like Cumbersome's voice, but dry as if his throat just needed a good cough to clear it.

"A *small* hero," James said.

"A small hero," mused the abbot aloud, "would not eat much."

"I haven't eaten anything ... *today*," James said.

"We can remedy that," the abbot said. He rang a small bell on the table, and a man—not Father Joseph—stuck his head in.

"Your eminence?" he asked.

"Some milk and some porridge for this boy. And one of your apple buns."

"Very good, sir," the man said, and shut the door.

Abbot Aelian cocked his head to one side and considered James. "Are you offering yourself as the small hero, young duke? That I cannot allow."

"Oh, no, not I," James was quick to assure him. "I don't have the courage for such ... such an undertaking."

A ghost of a smile flittered across the abbot's face but did not reach his eyes. "That is not the information I received about your work today in the orchard, my son. A false modesty is no modesty at all."

"Not modesty at all, sir. It was no courage I had. I gave it no thought at all. I just had to get my pony away from the unicorns. Did you know they have *very* sharp horns? One of them unseated the knight."

"Ah." There was that ghosting smile again. "I wondered about that. He didn't come back for his dinner."

James didn't hear the abbot's reply. He was too busy trying to think of a way to explain what he meant. And then it came to him.

"Sir Abbot, in my father's land there is a hero named ..." He hesitated again, then went forward boldly. "Sandy." But his face reddened as he said it.

"An odd name for a hero," remarked the abbot, somewhat suspiciously. "The others have been called things such as Sir Humphrey Hippomus of Castle Dire and Sir Sullivan Gallivant of the Long Barrow."

"And a very, uh, odd hero," agreed James. "But surely an odd hero would choose an odd name. Like Lochinvar and Bradamont and ..." He tried to remember the ballad heroes, but that was all he could come up with at a moment's notice. "I could write Sandy ... and ... ask for help."

"Nonsense, child, I will write. But it is less than a month before the unicorns will be gone—along with all our apples. If this hero doesn't come soon and save us ..."

"Begging your pardon, Lord Abbot," said James, "but I don't think Sandy will come if *you* write. Sandy is very, um, *particular*."

"Too *particular* for an abbot?" Abbot Aelian rubbed a long, elegant finger along his nose. "This Sandy would not be of a devilish nature?"

"Oh, no, sir," James said, shuffling his feet. "Not devilish at all. Only, um, different."

"I will think on this, but I am not certain," the abbot said. "You may go now to my dining room and have some food. But, James, no more disappearing for an entire day. Or jousting with the unicorns without my leave. I have not the courage to face your dear mother."

"Yes, sir," James said, doubting both the abbot's lack of courage and his mother's dearness to the old man.

The abbot waved James out the study door.

He went to the abbot's dining room, took the apple bun and left the rest, and ate it happily on his way back to the dortoir.

When he popped his head into the monks' dining room, he was relieved to find a plate of green vegetables waiting for him, and all ten of the boys. As James ate the vegetables greedily, the boys introduced themselves around the table and asked if he would like to listen to stories that night with them.

"Brother Daffyd is a wizard at telling tales," the boy called George told James.

"He knows hundreds of them. Maybe thousands," Aiden added.

Then redheaded Bartholomew said, as if conferring a great honor on James, "You can have the second choice of story, after me."

James kept on eating and nodded without comment. But new questions ran through his mind.

What was the full agreement the abbot had with his mother?

Why had the Green Knight forgone his free dinner?

What would Alexandria think of all this?

At the thought of Alexandria, and how she would have answered his questions or led him by the hand into the library to find out what she did not already know, the homesickness took hold again and shook him like a barn cat shakes a rat, till he felt it down in his bones.

He looked at the boys around the table waiting eagerly for his answer. But when he spoke, it was directly to Bartholomew, who was clearly the leader. "I think I am too weary after that fight with the unicorns. Can I listen to the stories another night?"

Bartholomew stared at him as if looking for a hidden meaning in James' words, some insult, but at that moment James yawned, quickly covering his mouth with the back of his right hand.

"Right. That kind of battle can take it out of you," Bartholomew conceded. "Took it out of your cape, too. Give it over to George here. He's good at darning and will have it fixed for you by morning."

When George looked ready to protest, Bartholomew gave him a look and swatted him with an open hand. "Do it!" he warned.

George's protest died unsaid, and he reached out for James' cloak.

James shrugged out of the garment and only then realized how rent and torn it was. All of a sudden, he began to shake. If the unicorn horns had come even a hand's span closer, he could have died.

He rose from the table on shaky legs. "Thank you, George," he said, not realizing how much he sounded like his uncle talking to the gardener or the stableman. Then before his knees could buckle, he walked out of the dining hall and headed towards his room and his small cot.

12

IN WHICH JAMES NOTICES HOW TIME FLEES

The very next morning, having gone over the abbey's accounts one last time, Abbot Aelian summoned James from the scriptorium, where he was beginning his study of Greek.

The sallow-faced monk who came with the message looked down at James, who was hard at work on the new alphabet, which was much trickier than the one he already knew. Hebrew, he'd been warned, would be the hardest of the lot, and so was to be left to the last.

The monk said with a scowl, "Himself wants to see you."

James looked up. He didn't know the name of this monk, nor did he much like his looks. Besides, he hated being brought out of his concentration. "Himself?"

"The abbot," the monk said sourly. "Who else?"

Who else indeed, James thought, and set the piece of practice scroll aside. He said nothing more to the monk, or the monk to him. Was he being summoned because he'd broken some new rule of the monastery and was to be scolded or put on bread and water, as his uncle had said would happen?

Or—he suddenly hoped—*maybe I'm being sent home?*

He squared his shoulders and stood, because he knew that, being a Callander, whatever the reason he'd been summoned, he'd do his duty, because that's what a Callander did.

Still, he didn't dare question the monk, just wrapped the newly darned cloak around him. George had done a very good job setting

in patches, for it turned out that his father and brothers were all tailors, and he had learned as a small boy to sew a fine seam before being sent to the monastery as an oblate.

James followed the bleak, brown-robed presence across the lawn and through the palace's front door.

He wasn't sure what to expect.

Abbot Aelian was sitting by the fire in a pillowed chair, a prayer book in his hand.

When the sour-faced monk cleared his throat, the abbot looked up, stuck his left pointer finger on the page of the book to mark it, and dismissed the monk with a wave of his right hand.

The bleak monk turned and left.

Then the abbot gazed for a long moment at James.

James felt that all his virtues and faults were being calculated and balanced.

Finally Abbot Aelian said, without any greeting or preamble, "Very well, James ... write to this hero, Sandy. You *do* know how to write?"

"Oh yes, Father Abbot," said James, relieved that he was not being scolded for anything.

The abbot waved him off as well, turning back to his prayer book, and James opened the heavy door and went back to the scriptorium, his heart singing in his chest like Great Tom, the abbey's bell that tolled the hours.

He found Brother Anselm in the scriptorium storeroom, counting out the unused scrolls.

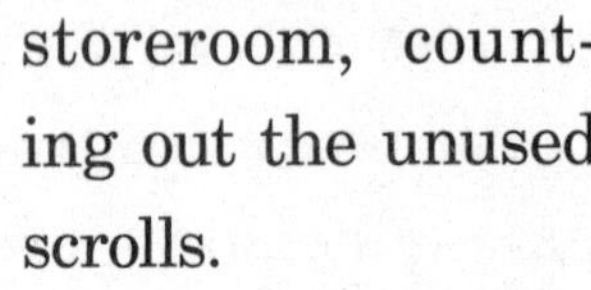

"Abbot Aelian has set me the task of writing a letter to my household at Castle Callander. I will need a bit of paper, a quill and dark ink, and—"

"Slow down," Brother Anselm said. He never moved or spoke quickly. Indeed, he was so round, James worried he would roll rather than run anytime he was called on to hurry.

James repeated the message, but more slowly.

"Are you certain?" Brother Anselm asked. "I only question this because you still have many months of practice ahead of you. And writing letters to go outside the abbey is what Brother Malcolm does. He has the best hand."

"It's a request to a particular hero that we house in Callander," James said carefully, slowly, and suddenly conscious that here in the house of the Lord he was doing a lot of... improvising.

That troubled him. But only a little. The destruction by the unicorns, and the possible destruction *of* the unicorns, troubled him more.

After a long pause, Brother Anselm asked, "Ah, well—a large letter or a small one?"

James thought a minute. The monks were very careful of their paper, which was precious. And this letter didn't need to be long. Or done in large italics. Just written persuasively. And done soon.

"Quite small, Brother Anselm," he said. "Almost a note."

"Good lad," Brother Anselm said, and found him a small piece of vellum that had been scraped once or twice and had a jagged edge.

James sat down at the desk and first gave a great deal of thought about what he needed to say in the letter before he ever dipped the quill into the ink pot. Only after he had the words completely in mind did he begin writing. Even with his careful planning, the letter was still full of ink blots because—while he knew his alpha and omega—his calligraphy, as Brother Luke had said, was a long way from being perfected yet.

But the blots and spots did not bother him. He knew italics, and a smattering of Latin, and was learning Greek. And though no one much answered his questions, the ones he had now were so much more important than any he had ever asked at home, and he was beginning to figure them out on his own.

And besides, he thought, putting false modesty aside, *my courage really has been tested. And I have even convinced an abbot to do my bidding.* In just two short weeks, he had grown years older. He was sure of it.

He read the letter over.

When the abbot read the letter, he actually smiled and remarked, "Very concise and to the point, though you are not an actual brother of the abbey yet, nor—as the heir to the dukedom—will you be allowed to do so. Also, you have misspelled my name. But, I admit, it is a difficult one." The smile that had so quickly come was gone by the end of his speech.

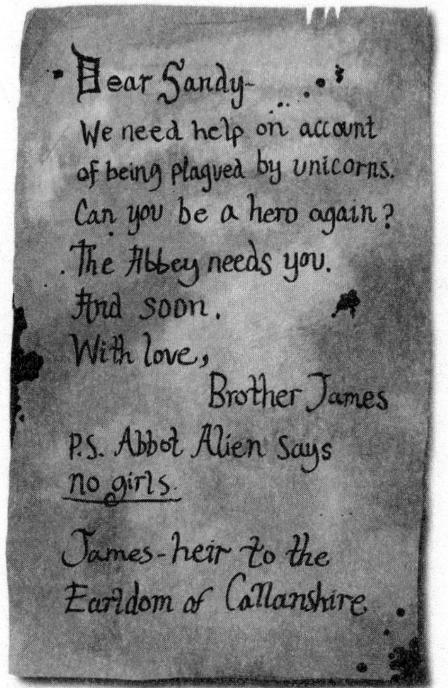

Dear Sandy-

We need help on account of being plagued by unicorns.
Can you be a hero again?
The Abbey needs you.
And soon.
With love,
Brother James
P.S. Abbot Alien Says no girls.

James-heir to the Earldom of Callanshire

The letter was sent by a courier monk on one of the two

horses in the abbey's stable. James wondered how long it would take for the hero to get the letter, how long for the hero to come to Cranford. Time mattered. Or, as one of Alexandria's Latin mottoes said, *Tempus fugit.* Time flees.

And then he put those thoughts aside and went back to perfecting his Greek and italic.

13

In which the hero Sandy arrives and faces the unicorns

As James learned later, it took the letter two and a half days to get to Castle Callander, for the courier monk rode dawn to dusk and ate as he rode.

As soon as he delivered the message and received a packet of food from Cook, he rode the two and a half days back. So he told Abbot Aelian, who passed the word along to James.

Then it took the hero Sandy nearly three days to prepare for the journey.

It took four days on the road, because along

the way Sandy had to rescue a maiden from an angry dragon of a would-be husband.

The maiden was not *really* in danger, only having an argument with her husband-to-be. Sandy counseled putting off the wedding until they could talk things through.

The maiden then suggested marrying Sandy instead.

That's when Sandy suddenly discovered an actual nearby dragon that needed dispatching—or so it was said—and after that a marauding giant in the next kingdom to contain. Well, a very big man, anyway, who had a score to settle with the king.

By then the maiden and her almost husband had talked things through and gotten married, much to the later regret of both of them. The dragon—who looked a lot like a crocodile brought back from the Crusades—was dispatched to the next kingdom, where he got a moat of his own. The giant was taken to a priest who held an exorcism, which helped the giant give up his addiction to marauding. Then he and the king made up, and in turn the giant helped with the church's soup kitchen.

It was, all in all, a fine hero's day.

But that's why it wasn't until a full week had gone by—a full week where the unicorns had done their worst on the apple trees before retiring for their week of digesting and their further week of excreting—that James' small hero Sandy entered the courtyard of Cranford Abbey.

James had been watching through the window every day since sending the letter, waiting for Sandy to arrive. He'd neglected his lessons. His Latin had suffered and likewise his Greek. And his calligraphy had not improved one whit since he'd written to ask for help.

Brother Luke was not pleased, nor was the abbot. Bartholomew and his crew teased James unmercifully about everything from his white-gold hair to his name. (Evidently "Callander" sounded so much like *calendar* that they said he was pitted like dates, and was a weakling as well.)

But James kept to his watch, waiting until

he saw the great barrel-chested white horse with the forelock plaited with a red ribbon, and the hero in armor sitting atop the horse in the abbey garden. He ran from the dortoir shouting, "Sandy! Sandy!"

"Hush, Brother James," said Sandy, dismounting and speaking in a remarkable tenor voice more suited to a bard than a fighting man. "I came as soon as I could."

Forgetting he was supposed to be learning monkish ways, James ran into the hero's arms.

"There, there," said Sandy, rubbing James' head with unrelenting knuckles, "I missed you, too."

At that moment, Abbot Aelian appeared.

"Sir," said Sandy, executing a remarkably fluid bow for someone in full armor, "I have come to do you service. I will rid you of this plague of unicorns."

The abbot was impressed because Sandy's armor was burnished by dragon's fire and dented in odd places from battles. "If you can do that, you are welcome indeed to have dinner with me this evening."

"Thank you, but no, my lord abbot," said Sandy. "I will stay here within the garden walls till the deed is done. That's how I work. Apart and alone." Another bow, and then Sandy remounted the white horse.

James turned to the abbot. "May I camp out with Sandy?"

"*Non licet*," said the abbot sternly. "It is not allowed."

"May James be my messenger?" asked Sandy. "And my helper?"

"*Certes*," said the abbot. "Yes, certainly."

"*Gratia, domine*," Sandy said—Latin for "Thanks, Abbot."

If the abbot was surprised the hero spoke Latin, a language not usually known to knights, only monks, well-bred ladies, and scholars, he didn't mention it. As it had been a long, hard season of heroes who had asked for much and given nothing in return but unwanted advice, Abbot Aelian was not about to make a fuss.

So the hero Sandy stayed in the orchard, creating a series of high wooden pens and gates of oak, and then making a maze out of rowan boughs, that most magical of woods.

James helped carry the wooden staves and dig postholes, and at the last festooned the palings with bright golden ribbons that had been blessed with holy water. He never minded the hard work—so hard, in fact, that he and Sandy had little time for conversation.

Building the pens and gates took a full week, building the maze a week more.

Brother Gregory, the cook, brought out their meals, staying only a moment to wonder at the small hero who was even smaller without armor and helm. Sandy labored in a strange mixture of a gardener's trews, a long shirt and tunic, and a cape that nearly touched the ground, despite the warmth of the mid-autumn.

Each day at noon, Abbot Aelian came to check the progress, and each time he asked, "Will you dine with me tonight?"

"*Non licet*," Sandy answered each time. "It is my promise to God that I stay apart and alone. If I break such an oath, I will get no help from above." Sandy pointed a finger at the sky.

Abbot Aelian crossed himself and left, pleased with the pens and maze but puzzled, too. They looked sturdy enough for perhaps one unicorn, but not an entire herd.

"Please bless this hero," he muttered under his breath as he left.

As for James, he was so pleased to have Sandy there, a reminder of home, that he worked extra hard at his studies in the evening, and soon caught up to the other boys in Latin and Greek, and was far ahead of them in developing a fine calligraphic hand as well.

As for the orchard, it looked ready for a feast rather than a war.

14

In Which James Witnesses the Battle of the Maze

Summoned by James, who knocked on the palace door, the abbot went out at once to see Sandy, who waited for them in front of the finished maze.

"The unicorns are coming, hero," said the abbot.

"I have heard them these three nights already," Sandy told him. "They are restless and hungry."

"You heard them because you're a hero?" asked James.

Sandy laughed. "I heard them because

I have been sleeping on the ground, little monk, little brother, while you are on a cot in the dortoir."

"What do you need from me?" asked Abbot Aelian.

"Only that you keep the monks and priests and all the oblates indoors," Sandy said. "A hero's business can be complicated by well-wishers and onlookers who get in the way and have to be rescued themselves."

"I will personally shut them in," said the abbot. "*Intellego omnes*"—Latin for "I understand all."

"I believe you do," said Sandy.

The abbot took James by the hand and led him away, something he had never done before, and he did not look back.

But James did, his palm cold in the abbot's hand, his worry written large on his face.

The unicorn herd arrived at daybreak the next morning as the canonical hour of Lauds was rung in by Great Tom. They came in a parade of trotting silver hooves, swirling silver manes, and spiraling horns. They pranced and pirouetted, making strange bleating sounds, their hooves kicking in the air.

Sandy stood in the center of the orchard maze, spear raised in both hands overhead, waiting.

The great lead stallion cried out a challenge, the sound somewhere between the whinny of a horse and the blat of a goat. Then he rose on his hind legs and sniffed the air.

Sandy began to sing in a lilting tenor voice:

Thread the maze,
Find the maid,
Seek the hero
Unafraid.

Bend your neck,
Bend your knee,
Come to me,
Come to me.

When the last note of the song ended, the unicorns suddenly leaped like goats, high over the stone walls into the garden, their hooves never even touching the rocks.

Capering, almost dancing, they began to thread the maze. The wind blew the golden ribbons that James had tied onto the palings till they were like banners in the air.

It was not the holy water on the ribbons nor the magic of the rowan boughs that called the unicorns in, but the song that Sandy sang.

James wondered, *Is it magic? An incantation? A wizard's spell?*

Whatever or wherever the song came from, the unicorns came into the maze as if pulled there by a golden thread. Head to tail to head to tail, they paced through the maze as though enchanted, as if they'd been tamed. They didn't stop to graze or nuzzle the remaining windfalls of apples; instead they crowded into the center pens and waited till their leader, the great stallion, marched right up to the hero.

Sandy stood still in full armor, back against a tree so laden with golden apples, they draped over the armor like a golden robe.

The stallion pointed his horn at Sandy's chest but did not thrust forward. Nor did

Sandy pierce him with the spear. Instead, hero and unicorn gave twin sighs and sank down together at the foot of the tree, the unicorn's head resting in Sandy's lap.

Gently, Sandy removed a yellow ribbon from the spear head and tied it halter-like over the stallion's nose, under his chin, pulling his white forelock through, braiding it quickly into a lover's knot.

The stallion's eyes, the color of antique gold, closed as Sandy began to sing again, so quietly only the two of them could hear.

When the song was done, Sandy pushed the great beast's heavy head away and stood, pulling him up at the same time. Then together, hero and beast walked back through the maze, the rest of the unicorns following docilely behind.

They went down the road till they were lost in the bright sunlight, till those who watched through the window slits—though they'd been warned against it—thought the hero and the herd had disappeared into heaven itself.

But James knew differently.

And so did the abbot.

Heaven would not have held either Sandy or the unicorns long in any case. But a stronger pen or a farther shore could. Sandy would lead the unicorns to a safe haven, not heaven, though it might mean many days and weeks of travel.

In the early evening, well after the bell rang for Nones, James was summoned once again to the abbot's palace. This time he wasn't worried about any punishment or blame. He wasn't worried that he'd done anything wrong.

This time when the abbot was sitting again by the fire, there was another chair, a smaller chair, pulled up next to his.

Without preamble, the abbot asked, "What do you think about the disappearance of the beasts?"

James liked that it was the abbot asking questions of him, not the other way around.

"The unicorns," he said thoughtfully, "may be gone this fall. But they *could* come back the next."

The abbot nodded. "Fine answer."

James swelled inside with pride, but he knew that he was close to a sin. So he didn't show on the outside any bit of it.

"I am certain," the abbot said to James, "that Sandy will return if needed."

Neither one of them spoke for some time, but the fire did, spitting out a crackling response they both ignored.

The abbot's eyes closed and his head slumped down on his chest. If he was breathing at all, it was hard to tell.

For a moment James wondered if he should call for one of the priests. Or the infirmerer. But before he had to make that decision, the abbot's eyes fluttered open. "Your hero left the white horse behind."

"Yes," James said, his face a sudden misery. "Its name is Carrywell. I expect the hero worried about its safety."

"A good name for a horse," said the abbot carefully.

James' lower lip trembled. "A good horse, too."

"I think the horse needs to go home," the abbot said. "Can you manage?"

James' face dared to show some hope. "Yes," he breathed. "Oh, yes."

"Word came this morning that your uncle has taken a bad turn. Your mother needs you. She has sent a pair of soldiers to escort you back."

James' face was suddenly wreathed in smiles. Not because his uncle was sick. He would never have wished for such a thing. But because he was about to go home.

"Yes," the abbot continued, "your mother needs you and so, I think, does your sister. When you see her, give her my thanks."

"My ... sister?" Smiles all gone, James looked at the abbot, trying to read his face.

"The hero," the abbot told him. "Sandy. She will need her horse—and her brother—when she gets home with that herd." He smiled. It made his face look years younger.

James took a deep breath, then let it out slowly. "*Certes*," he said, because he was a quick learner.

A smile almost played about the abbot's lips. "Before you go, I have something to show you."

"What is it?" asked James.

"It is called a telescope," said the abbot, "an instrument for seeing long distances. It was made by a Hollander man from a description in a book by our own John Dee."

James had heard of John Dee, the queen's magician, and said so, adding, "Isn't he of . . . a devilish nature?"

"*Not* a devil and not really a magician," said the abbot, "though he may seem so to those who do not understand science." He got out of his chair carefully, as if his bones were made of stained glass and might shatter. "But with this telescope, I shall show you a marvel."

The abbot led James over to the window, where a strange metal object pointed up to the sky. "Put your right eye here," he said to James, "and close the other."

James did as he was told, and a huge circle, the color of an old gold bangle that his mother had on a chain, a gift from his father, sprang into view.

"The moon," said the abbot.

James took another deep breath and looked closely. "Not cheese at all, then."

"*Certes*," the abbot said, and made a sound deep in his chest as if the sea were laughing.

At that, James laughed with him, happy for the moon, happy for the hero, happy for the unicorns, and most of all, happy for the promise of home.

AFTERWORDS

James *did* get home, and was embraced so long by his mother, he almost suffocated in her arms. She wept an ocean onto his collar, and asked his forgiveness for sending him away. “I listened to my brother when I should have been listening to my son.”

“But I learned so much at the abbey,” he told her. “Some Latin, some Greek. How to write in italic. And I want to learn more.”

“So you shall, my brave boy. The abbot has told me everything.”

Alexandria the Hero, with the herd of unicorns, came home as well, seven days after her brother. She and the beasts had stopped in other orchards along the way, and in meadows filled with milleflowers. They had to stay away from the roads. Besides, Alexandria was walking and singing to the stallion. Her voice was harsh from the seven days.

Their father, with a right leg that would never again work as well as the left, came home from the Holy Land the next season. He had spent nearly a year in a terrible prison, which was why he had disappeared for so long and had never written.

So James didn't have to worry about becoming the duke until many, many years later.

But when he *did* become duke, he was a thoughtful one like his father and a kind ruler like his mother. He always listened carefully to the questions the people of his shire asked and made careful and considered rulings in law. He was a strong steward of the land, which contained all that his father had left him, especially the hardy grove of golden apple trees—the seeds of which had been a present from a grateful abbot.

Uncle Archibald left Castle Callander to

become a priest at Cranford Abbey. There he experimented with the golden apple seeds, planting and tending dozens and dozens more Hosannah trees for many years. He and the abbot became best of friends and spent long evenings discussing plants and herbalries, which they wrote together. When he was too old to work in the fields anymore, Father Archibald wrote a treatise on the care of golden apples, while the abbot wrote his own masterwork on the feeding of unicorns.

But it was James, and his children after him, who were the careful shepherds of the herds of unicorns that fed contentedly on the Callander apples. The children were allowed to ride on the unicorns' backs, as long as they wore helms made especially for them by the castle blacksmith, and the unicorns tolerated them—and only them—to ride.

James founded and funded a local college in association with the abbey, a college in which history, literature, illumination, Bible studies, and especially science, were taught.

As for James' hero sister, Alexandria, when not off on an adventure, busily saving princesses—as well as princes—from a variety of wild beasts, she had a home with James and his family for as long as she lived, which was very long indeed.

LOOKING FOR MORE FROM THIS AUTHOR?

To connect with her visit
www.JaneYolen.com

ZONDERkidz